I0731753

# BAREFOOT KISSES

KRISTA LAKES

ZIRCONIA PUBLISHING, INC.

## ABOUT THIS BOOK

Lena Masterson was having a rough day.

Her coffee pot exploded, her favorite heel broke on the way to work, her computer died, and her coworker sabotaged her performance review that she should have aced. To top it all off, she had to stay late to fix someone else's mistake. So when she literally ran into a handsome stranger at work, she was fairly certain that it might actually be the worst day of her life. Instead, it was the start of something wonderful.

From the moment she nearly bowled the man over, she couldn't take her mind off of him. She didn't know anything about him, and could only assume that he was someone's assistant. Still, the encounter left her with new self-confidence. She made a move assertive enough to get the attention of her boss' boss, and be granted a new position as the personal paralegal of the head partner. This promotion soon led to an important trip to the Caribbean, where she saw a familiar face on the beach...

Everything seemed perfect when she was in Aiden's

arms (other than her missing shoe), but he was holding something back. Worse, Lena was keeping a secret from him as well. She knew that she couldn't keep up her little white lie forever, but it turned out that Aiden's secret was much bigger. *Much much much* bigger. A billion times bigger, in fact. Even though he treated her like Cinderella at the ball, it was possible that the billionaire playboy just thought of her as one of his "flavors of the week". After saying goodbye with one last barefoot kiss and returning to the real world, there was a burning question on Lena's mind: *Did this Prince Charming love her as much as she loved him?*

He brushed hair from my face and back behind my ear. I loved that he did that. It made me feel cherished. "You are so beautiful."

I looked up, my guilt melted by the heat in his eyes. Want made his gaze burn and set my soul aflame. He kissed me again, this time slower and with more purpose. His tongue infused raw desire straight into my mouth. He reached for my shirt, lifting it easily up over my head.

I moaned his name against his kiss as the shirt cleared. "I thought we were fishing..." I murmured as his hands caressed the fabric of my swim top, my nipples hardening and responding to his touch.

He nibbled on my shoulder, sending heat straight down my spine and to my core. "I can stop if you want..."

"No, no, no... don't stop," I gasped as he put his mouth to the delicate skin of my neck and sucked. He smiled against my skin. I bit my lip and looked out across the water. There wasn't a soul for miles, but the idea of doing it out in broad daylight had a delicious naughtiness to it...

～

Don't forget to sign up for my newsletter! You'll be the first to see my new covers, comment on new books of mine, and always know when books are available for free or on sale!

# CHAPTER 1

*C*offee dripped down the walls of the kitchen and spattered across the linoleum floor.

I stared at my brand new coffee pot in horror as it continued to spew boiling hot brown goo everywhere. This was not a good way to start the morning.

I scampered across the small kitchen, hiding behind a dishcloth and praying the coffee rain wouldn't land on me to pull the plug. The machine gurgled and died.

This was not a promising start to my morning.

I quickly cleaned up the walls and floor, hoping my roommate wouldn't attempt to use the cursed machine when she woke up. I made sure to leave Mindy a note, but she had a tendency to forget I existed. Sometimes, I was sure she thought a magic house fairy just came through to clean and add new supplies. Part of me almost hoped she would try the new machine without reading my warning. Either way, I would have to talk to her later about how she threw out the coffee pot box with the receipt in it without checking with me first.

I sighed and headed to the shower. Since I didn't have

the box to return the damn thing, I would have to find a way to make it work. Today was a day to make things work. I would figure something out. I always did. Nothing, not even a lack of coffee was going to stop me.

Today was my job review and I was going to rock it. As a paralegal for one of the biggest law firms in Chicago, I spent more time in the office than I did at home. I loved my job and I was damn good at it. I was respected by the lawyers I worked with and I had more lawyers requesting my work than any other paralegal in the firm. My job review was guaranteed to be good.

My sister and I already had reservations at a fancy restaurant to celebrate my raise that evening. I could hardly wait. Just a shower and an easy work day stood between me and my raise. I would be able to afford a new coffee pot if things went the way I was expecting.

The shower water turned on cold and stayed that way. Mindy must have forgotten to pay the gas bill again. I stared at the icy sheets of water and shivered. This wasn't a day I could skip a shower, so I counted to three and dove in.

It was the quickest shower of my life.

On the upside, the fact that it was such a quick shower and didn't make any steam, I was able to curl my hair in a relatively easy manner. I even managed not to burn myself. I put on my best suit, my favorite heels, and checked my makeup one last time before heading to work. *See*, I said to the girl in the mirror, *today is going to be good.*

I should have known better.

The train ride to downtown Chicago was relatively uneventful. It was late September and the weather outside promised to be a wonderful fall day. The sun was just beginning to tip up over the metal skyscrapers and warm the sidewalk below when I stepped off the train.

And then it started to rain.

I ran for the lobby of my building, holding my shoulder bag over my head in a futile attempt to shield my hair. Two steps from the main door, the rain stopped. I smiled until I caught my reflection in the window. The thirty seconds of rain had destroyed the curl in my hair and speckled my suit. All my hard work from this morning was ruined.

*It's not the end of the world,* I told myself, pulling my now flat hair up into a ponytail. I walked across the crowded lobby to get on the elevator. A nice man from two floors down held the door for me to squeeze into the elevator before it left the lobby. Someone tried to take my spot, jostling me to the side, and I stepped on the space for the elevator door and heard a small crack.

I stepped back to try and figure out the noise and the shiny metal doors slid shut without me inside. I would just have to wait for the next one. I took a step back and stumbled like a drunk. The cracking noise I heard had been my heel of my shoe snapping in two. The heel was now completely missing off of one shoe.

Not only were these my favorite pair of dress shoes, they were the only shoes I had brought with me. I stared down at my lopsided feet. This was not how this day was supposed to go. This was supposed to my day to shine and so far, all I had to show for it was no coffee, flat hair, and a broken shoe.

*I can still do this*, I told myself. *Things will get better.*

The law firm of McDonald, Smith and Ward spanned two floors of the Chicago Tower. The 16th floor was where the partners and senior associates wooed clients while the 15th floor was fondly referred to as "The Dungeon." The Dungeon was were the paralegals, secretaries, legal assistants, and new associates all worked with dreams of someday moving upstairs. If today went well, I would be on my way to moving up there.

After finally arriving on the fifteenth floor, I went about my work as usual, trying my best to ignore the fact that my shoe was irreparably damaged and hair wet. I smiled as I handed back files to lawyers and picked up new assignments. I kept on smiling even when two lawyers yelled at me for giving them bad news about their cases. I knew they weren't mad at me, but at the information. I tried not to let it phase me and went back to my desk.

My office was really just a table that I shared with several other paralegals. We all worked out in the open to give the lawyers easy access to us. I didn't really mind the setup, but I did wish I had a way to keep my pens from being stolen all the time.

I set up my laptop and went to work typing up a letter for one of the attorneys. It was tedious work and I nearly had it completed when I went to hit save. Instead of saving, the blue screen of death took over my computer.

*It's not the end of the world*, I promised myself as I dialed tech support. Tech support promised to send someone up right away as long as I stayed at my desk. I glanced at my watch. It was almost lunch time. My performance review was scheduled for after lunch and then I would be on my way to dinner with my little sister. The day still had so much opportunity.

"All this bad stuff is just so the good stuff will outweigh it later," I told myself as I sat patiently. I tried to work on other things, but my stomach was starting to growl. Just as I was about to give up on tech support and get my lunch, a very frazzled looking computer-guy arrived.

"Sorry, I'm new and I got lost on my way here," he apologized. "This place is a maze."

"It gets everyone turned around the first couple of times." With the way the cubicles and tables were set up, people were always getting lost. "I'm hoping you can save the file I was working on," I said handing him the computer. He began hitting buttons and with every passing minute, the frown on his face deepened.

"I'm really sorry, miss," he said, closing the lid and standing. "But, your laptop is toast."

I wanted to bang my head against the table. This was not my day.

"So there's no way to retrieve the letter I was working on?" I asked hopefully. The lawyer needed it in an hour. If I had to rewrite it completely, I wouldn't have time for lunch before my review.

"I'm really sorry, but no." The computer guy shook his head.

"What about the other files on there? I have a lot of work stored on that thing." Panic made my voice squeak a little. I had months of data and open cases on that computer.

"I'll be able to salvage that with some equipment in my office," he assured me. "Since this is a firm computer, I'll put it on a new laptop and bring it up for you. I'm afraid you'll have to use a loaner computer until I get that done, though."

"Thank you." I tried to sound grateful, but it was hard. I hated the loaner computers and now I was going to be spending my lunch working on one. He nodded and hurried away with my broken laptop. I got to work as quickly as I could.

I finished the letter and handed it off just in time to make it to my review. I went to Calvin's office and said a little prayer before knocking on his door. This was the part of my day that should make up for the crappy morning.

The door opened just as I raised my hand to knock and I nearly ended up knocking on Alexa instead of the door.

"Holy crap, Lena," Alexa shouted as she stepped back like I had actually hit her. "What's your problem?"

"I'm so sorry, Alexa!" I apologized, feeling my face blaze with color. "I was just coming to see Calvin."

She glared at me and smoothed her designer suit across her slim hips. Alexa Jones was fresh out of law school and for whatever reason, she hated me. Someone said I looked like the girl her fiance dumped her for, but I couldn't believe someone as educated as she was could be that shallow. All I knew was that she despised me.

"I'll see you later tonight, Calvin." Alexa gave Calvin a sweet smile before jostling me out of her way. She banged my shoulder against the door frame in the process, making me wince, but she didn't even look back.

As a paralegal, my review was with my supervisor, Calvin Abrams. He was a Jr. Associate who was expected to make the move upstairs to Sr. Associate by the end of the year. He was in charge of me and another paralegal, as well as the new hire associates. I liked him, and up until the time Alexa joined the staff, he had liked me.

For two years, I had been Calvin's go-to girl. Then, six months ago, Alexa had arrived and things changed between us. He stopped asking for me on his cases. I no longer went to court with him as a second chair. I was not a lawyer, and thus I suddenly was of no use to him.

"Come have a seat, Lena, and we'll get started," Calvin said, not looking up from his desk. I sat down cautiously, still blushing from nearly knocking on Alexa's face. He pulled out a file with my name on it and placed it neatly on the desk. "I'd like to make this as quick as possible for both of us."

I nodded eagerly and smoothed the stiff fabric of my skirt, but couldn't seem to get comfortable. Something about this meeting wasn't sitting well with me.

"I have some concerns about your performance, Lena." Calvin frowned at the papers in front of him. There was a tension in the room that shouldn't have been there. This was supposed to be an easy review with a pretty much guaranteed raise, but now I was getting nervous. "Alexa asked you to assist her with the Preston case discovery. She said you told her no, and that you weren't polite about it. It is your job to assist the lawyers here, Lena. I know you don't get along with Alexa, but if she asks you to do something, you need to do it."

I opened my mouth, but had nothing to say that would change his mind. It didn't matter that Alexa used me as her personal secretary. It didn't matter that I was already doing most of the work on all her other cases in addition to my other job duties because she didn't know how to do it properly. To be fair, I had snapped at her a little when she dropped the file for the Preston case in my lap. I was already behind with two other lawyers and it was her job, not mine. She just didn't want to do it because she had dinner reservations that night. I still couldn't believe she had brought it to Calvin, though. She tattled on me knowing my job review was coming up.

Calvin shuffled the papers on his desk before looking at me. His expression was the same as my father's when I had brought home a B- on my report card. I had gone from Calvin's favorite paralegal to problem child in his eyes. "I know you deserve this raise, but with what Alexa has said about your job performance with her, I can't in good conscience give it to you until you work things out with her.

And honestly, it makes me question putting your name into the partners for the scholarship."

"Calvin-" I started, but thought better of it and shut my mouth.

"I really wish you would be more like Alexa." Calvin looked at me with such disappointment and pity that I felt sick to my stomach. "You'll just need to work harder. Like she does. I can't take your name out of the scholarship running, but I will have to tell them my concerns.

It took everything I had not to get up and murder Alexa right then and there. That scholarship was my dream and I had worked my ass off for the law firm to be the top contender. I was already a part of every opportunity the law firm offered, but the full ride scholarship to Harvard Law was what I really wanted.

"Would you like to add anything, Lena?" Calvin asked. There was a lot I wanted to add, but none of it would help me get a raise or even keep my job. Several expletives and obscene offers sat on my tongue for what he could do with his opinion of me from Alexa.

"I don't feel that Alexa's assessment is unbiased or a good example of the rest of my interactions with staff," I said diplomatically. "If you look at the referrals written by some of the other lawyers, as well as my case numbers, you'll see that I've gone above and beyond the basic duties assigned to me. Mr. Joffrey's case, for example-"

"I don't care about Mr. Joffrey's case," Calvin replied, cutting me off. "Alexa's concerns still stand. If you can't work with one lawyer, how can I expect you to work with the others?"

I bit my tongue, nearly drawing blood. My file clearly showed that I *did* work well with the others. The other lawyers loved my work. I took a deep breath and tried to come up with a way to salvage this. There was always a way to salvage things. If I wanted to be a lawyer, I had to learn to manage situations like this.

"Mr. Abrams," I said slowly, using his formal title. "What do I need to do in order to prove to you that I am not only a reliable employee, but one of the best paralegals at this firm?"

He barked a laugh. "You may have the other lawyers willing to write nice things for you, but Alexa tells it like it is. I already told you, you need to be more like Alexa."

I wanted to scream. This wasn't anywhere close to fair. He wasn't listening to anything I had to say. I frowned trying to think of something to change his mind, but as I looked up at him, I realized it was a lost cause. He took Alexa's word as gospel.

"I see," was the only thing I could say.

"I hope to see you make some improvements." Calvin didn't look at me as he filed my review away in his desk. "You can go now."

I stood stiffly. My skirt pinched at my stomach and there was a run in my nylons. It took everything I had to turn and walk out with as much grace as a broken heel could give me. I looked back at him as I opened the door to leave and wondered how things could have gone so poorly.

## CHAPTER 2

*T*wo shimmering dust specks twisted through the golden evening sunlight, circling and spinning, dancing with one another like long lost lovers as they slowly descended and finally came to rest on the shiny black surface of my desk. There they sat, motionless and lifeless after their golden fall. I stared at them for a moment, wondering if motes of dust could feel, and if they could, if they felt as let down as I did.

I shifted in my chair, feeling the stiff fabric of my skirt tighten across my legs. I wished I had brought a change of clothes so I didn't have to wear my suit anymore. The lawyers were expected to dress in suits, but as a paralegal, I was allowed to wear business casual. I kicked at the broken pair of heels under my desk and tugged at my uncomfortable skirt. Right now, I would have killed for a pair of flats and pants.

My phone buzzed, skittering along the edge of my desk. I hoped it wasn't my sister canceling on me. We had dinner reservations, and while we were no longer going to be able to celebrate my raise, a drink sounded fantastic. Dinner with my little sister would at least make my day a little better.

The message was from Alexa. I thought about chucking my phone across the hallway instead of checking it, but since I didn't get the raise, I knew I wouldn't be able to afford a new one. I opened the message, my jaw falling a little bit as I read it.

*Go to my office and find the discovery file for the Preston Case. It needs to be in Calvin's office by 5.*

It was 4:45. I had fifteen minutes to go find the stupid file and give it to Calvin, and since she was asking me to do it, that meant she had left early. I was stuck doing her work again, and if I was late getting it to Calvin, it would be my fault. Anger burned hot in my throat. I had to do it or risk losing my job. Calvin would put Alexa over me every time because she was an associate and I was just a lowly paralegal.

I left my broken shoes tucked under my desk and crossed the hall to Alexa's office barefoot. No one was around, and there was no way I was wearing broken shoes if I didn't have to. Nylon stockings beat limping down the hall.

Alexa's office was tiny, but it was all hers. She never let me forget that she, as an associate, had a real office while I just had a desk that I had to share with the other paralegals. It was a good thing she didn't have to share with anyone, because it was a total mess. Files were strewn across the desk and stacked in haphazard piles. Books and more open files laid scattered across the filing cabinets on the back wall. I recognized some of the books as ones from the research library upstairs.

I picked up one, checking the title: *Wage and Hour Collective and Class Litigation*. This was part of the permanent reference section and wasn't even supposed to leave the library. I sighed and set it down. I was leaving it in her office. Alexa could deal with the trouble that was going to come down on her for having it.

As soon as the book left my fingers, I had a bad feeling about it. That was too easy. Alexa never got in trouble for things. Ever. Especially when it was her fault. I felt the need to check and make sure she wasn't going to screw me over. Again.

She had left her computer on, so it only took me a moment to log onto the law firm computer system to check the status of the book. It was checked out in my name. I had no idea how she even had my account number, but she had been using it for a while. She had not only taken two reserved books that weren't supposed to leave the library, but four others that were due at the end of the day. If Alexa didn't return them on time, which considering she wasn't even here to deliver her own files, I was the one who was going to get busted. I wouldn't qualify for even a cost of living raise with that on my head.

I collected all the books and stacked them on the edge of the desk while I searched for the discovery file. It took a little while, but I finally found it buried under two other files and a stack of magazines. Just holding it made my stomach boil with anger. It was the discovery information that she had tried to pawn off on me. This was the reason for my bad review.

It felt surprisingly light, so I thumbed through it to make sure all the pages were there. The file was complete, but pitifully short. I checked it again, just to make sure I wasn't missing something. Calvin was going to be pissed. This was a huge case, one that the head partners were involved in, and Alexa had completely half-assed it. She was supposed to have researched every aspect of our clients and their accuser, but just glancing through it I could see items that Alexa had completely skipped over to save herself time. The partners were not going to be happy about this. I really hoped that Alexa was in for some of the karmic justice she deserved.

"Whatever," I mumbled as I placed the folder on top of my stack of books. Before today, I would have considered adding in more research, but not anymore. My lips twitched up at the idea of him calling her and forcing her to come back and work on it tonight. I imagined her showing up in uncomfortable party clothes and having to work into the night as I skipped off to my fancy dinner. The look on her imaginary face made me smile.

All I had to do was drop the file off at Calvin's office, then head upstairs to return the books before I got in trouble for them. Once I had that done, I could text my sister to bring a spare set of shoes with her to the restaurant and I would be on my way to dinner. There was less than ten minutes left in my workday- what could happen in ten minutes that could ruin things further?

The stack of books was heavier than I had expected, and the file kept trying to slip off as I tried to open the door without dropping anything, but I was determined to get out of here on time. I finally caught the door handle and swung it open as hard as I could. I rushed out without looking so the door wouldn't slam shut on me before I could escape.

I should have looked, because instead of an empty hallway in front of me, there was a person. All I saw was his white dress shirt before I nearly barreled into him. I shrieked and nearly threw my hands up in the air in surprise. Luckily, I managed to keep the books in my arms despite my shock, but the file resting on top was not so lucky. It opened, sending the papers inside fluttering to the ground like snow.

"I am so sorry," I said quickly as I set my books down on the ground and began scrambling to pick up the pieces of paper. I was just glad I had managed not to injure either of us. "I wasn't looking where I was going, and-"

"It was my fault," the man assured me, handing me the file folder. He was down on one knee, helping me pick up the fallen reports. I looked up at him to see the most amazing hazel eyes I had ever seen in my life. Green, gold, brown, and just a touch of blue swirled together like granite under green water. Hair the color of honey with just a slight curl accented the colors of his eyes. He was smiling at me, and the smile in addition to those eyes made my heart skip a beat.

I tried not to stare, but he was possibly the most handsome man I had ever met in real life. His features were strong and bold, but chiseled and sophisticated. High cheekbones contrasted nicely with a strong, almost crooked nose. I wondered if he had broken it at some point in his life. It added character and mystery. He was simply breathtaking.

It took me a moment of staring before I took the folder from him. "Thanks," I managed to get out. I could feel my cheeks starting to burn so I looked down at his shoes instead of his face. They were expensive shoes. His gray dress pants were of high quality too, as was the cream-colored button-up shirt he was wearing. After working with incredibly high paid lawyers, I had learned to appreciate quality. His clothing was expensive, but practical. I had seen similar outfits on high paid personal assistants.

The body underneath those clothes was what really captured my attention. His broad shoulders and the muscles of his arms screamed that he enjoyed some sort of physical activity. Boxing maybe? That would certainly explain the nose. He didn't have a tie, so I figured he must be someone's assistant. Clients typically stayed up on the sixteenth floor and sent their assistants down to the Dungeon.

"Did I knock your shoes off?" he asked. I nearly dropped the file.

"What?" I gasped, feeling incredibly flustered. I hoped he thought the blush searing across my cheeks was from nearly running him over and not the way he was making my heart pitter-patter and my brain think dirty thoughts about him knocking my shoes off.

"You aren't wearing shoes," he explained. He had a deep voice that was easy to listen to.

"Oh, right!" I laughed nervously. I always had a hard time around handsome men. I never could tell what they were thinking. "I broke a heel earlier today, so I left them under my desk. I didn't think I'd run into anyone today."

He chuckled at my unintentional pun and handed me the last loose piece of paper. My hand accidentally brushed against his, sending a thrill straight up my arm and directly into my heart. I glanced up at his face, hoping to see the same reaction but he was already rising to his feet.

I quickly counted and organized the pages in the file to make sure they were all still there. For once I was actually glad Alexa had skimped on her work; it meant I had less to pick up. I turned to pick up the books, but the man already had them in his arms.

"Let me," he said, smiling at my confused expression.

"You really don't have to do that. I can get them," I replied, feeling incredibly self conscious as I rose from the floor. Only teenagers from the 1950's offered to carry a girl's books. "Besides, I was the one who ran into you."

"Then how about a trade?" he offered, keeping the books close to him so I couldn't take them. His eyes held a secret mirth, as though he knew exactly what I was thinking and found it amusing. "I'll carry the books for you if you'll show me how to get out of here."

"What?" I was saying that a lot to this man, but he had me thoroughly flustered.

"I'll carry the books for you if you show me the way to the main elevators," he explained. "That's why I was coming to your office. I've been wandering around looking for the way out when I saw the light on in there."

"The exit's actually just around the corner and to the right," I said, pointing down the hallway helpfully. "People are always getting lost down here. Someone really should have walked you out."

He flashed me a heart-stopping grin. I suddenly wished I hadn't just told him where the exit was. I should know better than to tell good looking men who want to carry my books how to escape from me.

"Then why don't you walk me out once we've delivered these?" he asked, ignoring my directions. For whatever reason, he wanted to carry my books. Maybe he just felt bad about nearly running me over.

"Okay," I said, tucking a stray strand of hair behind my ear. "I have to drop this file off at my boss's office before we take the books upstairs. You sure? You really don't have to."

"I'm sure," he told me, the corners of his mouth moving up toward another grin. "I'm waiting for my ride, and I would rather spend the time carrying your books than waiting in the lobby."

"It's over this way," I said, leading the way down the hall. I could feel him walking beside me, far enough away to be polite, but close enough that I was very aware of his presence. Plus, he smelled amazing. It was a clean, light scent that reminded me more of soap than cologne. The short walk to Calvin's office was not nearly long enough.

I knocked smartly on the door and Calvin answered. He had loosened his tie and looked overworked. His flat brown hair needed a trim and he looked pale as the afternoon light faded and the harsh florescent lights were all that was left. He glared at me with dark eyes as I handed him the file.

"Here's the discovery file from Alexa," I informed him. He snatched it from me and began going over it.

"Lena, this was supposed to be with me an hour ago. Kathryn's on my ass for this. You need to do your job." He glared at me, wanting to say more but noticing the man standing behind me. He wasn't about to make a scene in front of someone who could be a potential client. "We've talked about this."

"She just sent me the message to give it to you five minutes ago. I can show it to you if you'd like." I tried to keep my voice calm and even, though it was difficult. I wanted to snarl and snap that this was Alexa's fault and not mine, but I knew book-holding-man could hear every word and I didn't want to sound petulant in front of him.

Calvin frowned. His eyes focused on me and I could tell he wanted to berate me for being late, but couldn't with our observer present. "No. I'll take it up with Alexa." He turned the last page of the file and looked up at me, incredulous. "Where's the rest of it?"

For a moment, I panicked and thought I lost a page. But, I had counted twice, so I knew they had to be all there. He had to just be shocked that it was so short, especially since it was for such a big case. "That's all she gave me," I informed him calmly. Inside, my stomach was a bag of hot snakes.

Calvin's eyes darkened. If book-holding-man hadn't

been there, I would have been blamed and yelled at for something that wasn't my fault. I sent the man behind me a silent beam of gratitude for just being there.

"This isn't enough. Do you have any idea how big this case is? I need to get it to Kathryn tomorrow morning before we meet with the client. You'll have to stay late and add to it." Calvin shut the folder and crossed his arms. He seemed to stare over me, like I wasn't even worthy of his gaze.

"What!?" I squeaked before I could modulate my voice. This wasn't fair! "I have plans tonight. I have a date tonight! It was Alexa's job- make her do it!"

"Sorry, Lena. It's your responsibility now. Get it done." Calvin met my eyes. He was pissed and wanted to yell, but couldn't. He didn't know who the assistant behind me belonged to and he didn't want his name tarnished in the upper circles of the company. I opened my mouth to protest again, but he just shut the door in my face.

I stared at the wooden grain of the door for a moment, trying to understand how my day could have gone so terribly wrong. It was as if the universe were punishing me for something.

"Sorry about that," I said, turning around and putting a pleasant expression on my face. His face was unreadable and I refused to look at his eyes. I was too ashamed of how my boss had just treated me. "The elevator upstairs to the library is just around the corner. I can show you out now if you want, though. You don't have to go upstairs."

"I said I'd carry them," he replied, smiling gently at me. I looked up and again was lost in those beautiful eyes. When he looked at me, I felt like I was the center of his world. It was a heady feeling. The loss of his gaze was almost painful as he turned to walk in the direction I had just pointed. I hurried to catch up to him, feeling a deep gratitude for him not bailing on me. It was a sad statement that a stranger I had known for five minutes was the kindest person I had talked to all day.

"Thank you," I said catching up to him. I wanted to tell him just how much the simple gesture meant to me today, but I didn't want to sound crazy. He was just killing time until his ride got here, but his help was the nicest thing he could have done for me today.

"So, you had a date tonight?" he said conversationally as we walked. I was glad he wasn't commenting on how my boss had behaved or how my evening had been ruined.

"That's what you picked up on out of that conversation? My date?" I teased gently, pressing the call button for the elevator. He shrugged, his broad shoulders moving easily as he smiled crookedly. There was an easy sex appeal to him that made it hard to concentrate on anything but how good he made that shirt look.

I knew I looked terrible. My mascara had to be in raccoon territory and my dark blonde hair was falling out of the bun I had put it in after the rain. Plus, I was barefoot and my nylons were running. He was so far out of my league that I felt lucky just to be in the same building as him. A man as good-looking as he was didn't go for Plain Jane girls like me. They just flirted, beefing up their game and getting ready for the hotter girls. Like Alexa.

Even though I knew he couldn't possibly be actually interested in me, he still made my body react like I had a chance. Every part of me wanted him to know that I was a woman and very interested in the heat his gaze was giving off. Even if he didn't mean it, his smoldering smile was going to give me some wonderful dreams later.

"It was a date with my sister," I explained, stepping into the open elevator doors. He followed behind me, and I suddenly wished the elevator was smaller so we would have to stand closer together. "She was going to take me out to celebrate."

"What are you celebrating?" he asked. I pushed the button for the next floor up and hoped that the power would go out. I could happily spend the evening with this man in an elevator.

"I won a case." The lie came quick and easy. I didn't even actually think about it. I didn't want to tell him that we were supposed to celebrate the raise I didn't get in the review that had gone completely sour. I didn't want to embarrass myself anymore than I already had. Besides, it wasn't a total lie. I had worked on the case Calvin won yesterday, so technically, I had won the case too.

He smiled proudly at me and I felt all warm and fuzzy inside. "Congratulations!"

I liked the way he said it- like he meant it. It was the first nice thing anyone had said to me all day and it gave me a wonderful, heady joy. For a moment, my bad day wasn't bad at all.

"You have any other dates planned to celebrate it?" he asked as the elevator came to a stop. There was a cautious expectancy on the edges of his voice that my brain wanted to interpret as interest. He wanted to know if I was seeing anyone.

"No. No dates or anyone to take me on one," I replied, feeling brave with him. "Why? You planning on asking me out on one?"

"Maybe," he said with a shrug and a wry smile. I couldn't read his face well enough to tell if he was just flirting or serious.

The idea that he would even be interested in taking me on a date made my stomach do happy flip flops. My brain said he was joking because there was no way he was serious. I tried to think of a reply that wouldn't make me look overeager if he was just playing with me and couldn't. The elevator doors opened before I had to respond, and I gratefully hurried out before I said something that gave away how much I would enjoy a date.

I glanced behind me to see him still wearing a self-assured half-smile across his handsome face. I shook my head to clear my thoughts, but he was still dominating all my thinking power. I wanted him to be serious about wanting a date. I wanted it, but I wasn't sure I could handle it if I got one. A girl could fall in love with a man like that and never recover. Besides, who meets their Prince Charming in an elevator on a day when nothing seems to go right?

## CHAPTER 3

The upper floor of the McDonald, Smith and Ward law firm was made for impressing clients. It had a chic modern vibe that screamed wealth and power. The Chicago office was the flagship for the six other US branches and two international offices, and every inch was made to represent that fact.

Not far from the elevator was the legal library. While many firms were switching to strictly computer-based systems, McDonald, Smith and Ward had decided to use the beauty of the old books to impress clients. Big, sound-proof glass windows separated it from the hallway, but let anyone who walked past see the glorious amount of books inside. The collection was the envy of several small law schools.

I glanced over at my mysterious companion, watching for his reaction. He didn't have one. That told me two things. He had a boss that could afford my firm and that he had been here enough times that the opulence no longer effected him.

Darcie, the librarian, didn't look up from her computer as we entered her domain. "I'll be with you in just a second," she murmured. I knew her well enough to know she was lost in her own world researching something for an attorney.

"I just need to return some books Alexa checked out under my name," I told her as Book-man carefully placed the stack on the heavy wooden desk.

Darcie hit what must have been the save button and looked up, smiling as she recognized me. "Hi, Lena. How's your day going?"

"She won her big case," Book-man supplied when I hesitated. I felt my cheeks go bright red. Darcie was my best friend and would know that I had kind-of lied.

"You did, did you?" she asked innocently, looking at Book-man and then back at me with skeptical cornflower blue eyes. The corners of her mouth were twitching in an obvious attempt to keep from smiling. She was going to give me hell about this later. "Congratulations."

"Thanks Darcie," I replied, glad that she was going along with it in front of Book-man. She was a good friend. I pointed to the books. "I need to return these for Alexa."

Book-man looked back and forth between the two of us for a moment, evaluating if he wanted to stay in the conversation, and then stepped back from the desk and pretended to look at the books lining the walls. I knew he could still hear every word, but I appreciated the gesture of giving us space. Darcie winked at me as she picked up the first book and scanned it into the computer.

"It says they're checked out to you, not Alexa." Darcie frowned at the computer and double-checked the title of the book. Her voice grew cold. "This book isn't supposed to leave the library. I've been searching for it for two days."

"That's how you know it wasn't me. She must have checked them out under my ID number after hours." There were three things that Darcie Erickson loved: her husband, good food, and her books. I knew she and her husband were trying to add another little someone to that list, but it hadn't happened yet. Their lack of success seemed to only fuel her mothering tendencies toward her beloved books.

Darcie's mouth tightened into a thin line as she checked the rest of the books back in. The two of us had become friends the moment I had walked into the firm. She knew more about law and research than anyone I had ever met. I would often bring my work upstairs and sit at one of the research desks, feeling as if I could win any legal case given to me if I spent enough time with those books and Darcie.

"Alexa thinks she entitled to the damn world," Darcie mumbled as she checked in another book. I was glad she knew I would have never taken those books because she had murder in her eyes. She got along with Alexa about as well as I did. "I guess I should just be happy she even bothered to check them out at all this time. I'm going to change your account number so she can't do it again."

"Thanks, Darcie. I appreciate it," I said, feeling a little better. I wished Alexa would get in trouble for this, but even if Darcie reported it, it would end up being my word against Alexa's. Since Alexa was an attorney and I wasn't, she would win every time.

"Thank you for bringing them back," Darcie replied, putting the last book on her re-shelf pile. She patted the top one like a good child before leaning back in her chair to take a better look at Book-man. He was still looking politely at a shelf of books, but we had an excellent view of his very muscular backside. She mouthed the word, "Nice!" before speaking aloud. "All done. You have a great evening, Lena. And congratulations on your big case."

I stuck my tongue out at her before Book-man turned

around. She gave me a wide, cheeky grin in return. I knew in about thirty minutes she'd be texting me to see if she could get the scoop on why a cute guy was carrying my books to the library.

"Bye, Darcie," I said, glaring at her as I moved away from the desk.

"It was nice to meet you," Book-man added, holding the door open for me to walk out.

"You too!" came Darcie's reply just before the door shut behind us. The hallway was mostly empty, as anyone who was staying late was holed up in their offices.

"Thank you again. You really didn't have to carry the books," I told him once the door was officially shut. I could see Darcie inside, pretending to look at her computer but really just watching the two of us and grinning at me like a Cheshire cat.

"It was my pleasure," he replied warmly. "My name's Aiden, by the way." He extended his hand out to me for a handshake, which I took with a smile.

"I'm Lena." His grasp was firm and strong, and I didn't want to let go. Just touching his skin made the butterflies in my stomach start mamboing. I hoped I wasn't blushing too badly. If I kept this up, I knew I was just going to embarrass myself. I forced myself to let go of his hand and turn to start walking.

"So, what *are* you doing for dinner?" he asked, matching his steps to my slow ones.

"What do you mean?" I asked, a little confused. My mind was still on how Alexa could have gotten my ID number to check out the books, not on what I was going to eat in a few hours.

"Since your dinner plans were canceled, what are you doing for dinner?" He smiled at me, his eyes following me like I was made of light. I loved the way he looked at me.

"I actually don't know yet." I tucked the loose strand of hair behind my ear again. "Probably just eat the granola bar in my desk or something."

"A granola bar?" Aiden made a displeased face, as though I had said I was eating a cardboard box. "Not even pizza?"

"There's only so much pizza a girl can eat. I don't think I've had an actual meal that wasn't pizza or some sort of take out in well over a week. A granola bar actually sounds better than pizza right now," I explained. I could see the main lobby for the firm and tried to slow my steps even further without being too obvious. Talking with Aiden had been the best part of my day.

"They keep you that busy?" He raised his perfectly groomed eyebrows in appreciation. "You must be one of their best attorneys."

I smiled and looked down at my shoeless feet without correcting him. He thought I was a lawyer. I certainly was dressed like one today, he had found me in an attorney's office, and I had told him I had won a case. I didn't want to tell him that I wasn't actually a lawyer. I would probably never see him again, and it was nice to feel important for once. He saw me as someone significant, and after the way my day had gone, it felt good to be appreciated.

"Not really. I'm pretty low level." It wasn't a lie. I just wasn't correcting him. "I'm working my way up and that means long hours."

He turned and looked me over, appraising what he saw. "I have a feeling you won't be low level for long."

"Thank you," I said, feeling proud of myself for the first time all day. I grinned up shyly at him. He looked at me like he saw something worthwhile. I wanted this moment to last forever.

Despite walking as slow as I possibly could without crawling, we were at the main entrance to the law firm. It was time for me to say goodbye to my book-carrying hero and to go back to real life. I showed him past the big gray desk that dominated the lobby. The usual secretary had gone home for the evening, so the lobby was deserted and quiet. The silver elevator doors glared like giant eyes, staring at us as we approached.

"Here's the main elevators. They'll take you down to the main lobby and you should be able to escape the building from there," I said, slowing to a halt by the desk. Aiden stood close enough to touch, smiling at me as he prepared to say goodbye. My heart started to flutter at his presence, despite my best efforts to stay calm.

I had no idea how he had such an unnerving effect on me. He was just standing there, looking casual and relaxed, but he was making my heart pound like a school-girl. I suddenly didn't know what to do with my hands, but I couldn't find a place for them that didn't feel awkward. I wanted to become a lawyer and stand in front a jury, but standing in front of him with his eyes absorbing me, I was all aflutter and nervous.

"Thank you for showing me out," he said quietly, his voice filling the empty lobby with warmth. "I'm glad I met you. It made the trip to the lawyer's office worth while."

I blushed, and looked down at my bare feet with a smile, causing the loose strand of hair to fall across my face again. He reached his hand out and tucked it back behind my ear for me, raising my chin to look up at him in the process. His eyes drew me into him, pulling me into his orbit and making me forget everything else.

I thought he was going to kiss me. I stared at his perfect lips and wondering just how amazing it would feel to kiss him. There was a tension forming between us that was threatening to give off sparks if we didn't satisfy it. For one glorious moment in time, I was sure that he was going to lean forward, tip his head, and press his mouth against mine. I knew he would taste better than anything I could imagine and I wanted it. I wanted to kiss him, to touch him, to hear his voice all night long.

Just as I was closing my eyes to kiss him, my heart pounding and mouth ready, the elevator doors chimed their arrival. We both pulled back. The spell was broken. We were two strangers back in an empty law firm lobby who had no business even thinking of kissing one another.

"There you are, Aiden." A man that looked like a body-builder stepped out of the elevator. He was wearing a dark suit that fit him like a glove and a blue-eyed scowl that dropped the temperature of the room by three degrees. "I've been looking all over for you." The temp dropped another two degrees when he saw me standing so close to Aiden. He was all control and power. I could only think that he was Aiden's boss.

"Ben, this is Lena." Aiden replied calmly. Ben's scowl wasn't having the bone-chilling effect on him that it was on me. Ben's ice blue stare met Aiden's warm hazel one and the two seemed to hold a silent conversation with their eyes. Aiden didn't step away, yet it felt like there was suddenly a respectful distance between us. "She was kind enough to show me the way out after I got lost."

"It's very nice to meet you, Lena." Ben was pure professionalism and politeness as he extended his hand in greeting. His grip was just as strong as Aiden's but it didn't inspire the same breathless flutter in my chest. He released me and glared at Aiden. "We need to get going. We're going to be late."

Aiden glanced at his watch and nodded. "Of course." He turned to face me, a soft smile playing at his lips. Again, I wanted to kiss him, but I knew I couldn't. It seemed like he was in enough trouble with Ben for being late without me adding a kiss to his lateness. "Have a wonderful evening, Lena. Congratulations again on the case."

I smiled broadly up at him. "Thank you. For everything."

A full smile crossed Aiden's face before he walked away and joined Ben in the elevator. Ben pressed the button for their floor and Aiden's eyes met mine. We stayed that way for a breathless moment, holding me in his gaze before the elevator doors slid shut and took him away.

My knees wobbled and I realized I had forgotten to breathe. With a deep sigh, I ran my hand across my hair, smoothing it back and down. I didn't know it was possible to be that attracted to someone that quickly. I giggled and shook my head. A handsome man carrying my books and giving me compliments? He had certainly been the high-light of my day.

I leaned against the big gray desk for a moment, letting myself have the happy moment. I wished I could have kissed him. That would have made up for the terribleness of my day. Unfortunately, I didn't even know his last name or how to contact him again. That part certainly fit better with the overall tone of my day.

My phone chirped, letting me know I had another message. It was from my sister. She was excited for our dinner and wanted to know if she should wear her red dress or the black one. The happy feeling Aiden had inspired slowly melted away.

I knew I couldn't stay here all day, reliving my almost

kiss with the Handsome Book-man. I had to call my sister and tell her that I wasn't going to make it to dinner and start fixing more of Alexa's mistakes. I glanced back one last time at the elevator doors, hoping that they would open and he would be standing there, but they stayed shut. With a heavy sigh, I turned and headed back to work.

## CHAPTER 4

$\mathcal{M}$y chair squeaked as I leaned forward to look at the pictures coming up on my laptop screen. Technically, it was Alexa's chair but since she wasn't using it, I had claimed it and her office as my own for the evening. If I was forced to stay late to do her job, I might as well be comfortable in her office doing it. I had my laptop set up with notepad and pen as I searched for information on the individuals involved in the Preston case.

The case centered around a workplace accident and the plaintiff was suing our client for millions. He had been injured by company machinery and was suing Preston Corp for enough money to buy a small island. Alexa had done the crappiest job ever looking up the backgrounds of both parties. She had copied the Preston Corp information from Wikipedia and then barely checked the plaintiff's myFace page, let alone looked through his pictures or even found his blog. As I added pages upon pages of missed information to the file, I had to wonder just how the hell Alexa had ever gotten hired.

I clicked on one of the plaintiff's friends and starting

going through his pictures. What I found made me sit straight up in the squeaky chair. My stomach grumbled, but I didn't pay it any attention. I'd have that granola bar soon enough, but I wasn't interested in eating at the moment. It was very possible that I had just found something that would give our firm the slam-dunk on the Preston case.

Staring at me from the computer screen was the plaintiff hanging upside down from a piece of machinery. He wasn't tagged, but the picture was set to public. Anyone could view it. I clicked on the next picture to see him jumping off the roof of one of the fork lifts. The date on the picture matched the plaintiff's injury date.

Grinning, I started printing and saving the pictures as fast as I could. The key to the entire case had been under Alexa's nose the entire time. It had taken a little digging, but she should have found this. Millions of dollars and lots of bad publicity was on the line for our client and I had just found the evidence that would save them from all of it.

"See if Alexa blocks my raise this time," I said smugly to myself. I couldn't wait to see Calvin's face when I handed him this.

"So, you won your big case, did you?" Darcie asked, stepping through the open door of the office. I had left it propped open this time, hoping a little that maybe Aiden would find a reason to come back. Darcie wasn't Aiden, but she was a decent alternative.

I didn't look up from the computer as I clicked, saved, and printed the pictures. "Yup. I totally did." I was busted. She knew I had no big cases to win.

"And which case was that?" Darcie leaned against the door frame, false innocence coming off her in waves.

"The big one, obviously."

I could feel her roll her eyes at me. "You have so many big cases, I'm not sure which one you mean."

I stopped typing and looked up at her. "The one where an incredibly hot guy asked why I was going out to celebrate, and I didn't have the guts to tell him that I was supposed to go have dinner to celebrate the raise I didn't get." I shrugged to try and brush away the hurt. "Winning a case just sounded better."

"You didn't get the raise?" Righteous indignation filled her voice and it made me feel just a little bit better to know I wasn't the only one upset by it. "But you earned it! You put in more hours here than some of the attorneys!"

"I know." I smiled bitterly. "Remind me to thank Alexa later."

"Alexa gave you a bad review?" Darcie stomped over to the desk. I was slightly afraid she was going to pick up Alexa's stapler and throw it. "After all you've done for her?"

I plastered the biggest, most sarcastic grin I could muster and gave her two big thumbs up. "I have the greatest boss ever!" I didn't hold the smile long. "At least Louisa was still able to use the reservations. She went with her boyfriend instead."

"How is your sister?" Darcie asked, clearing a small corner of the desk and perching on the edge.

"She's good," I told her, turning back to the computer to finish my task. "She's loving college and being away from mom and dad. It's good for her. I'm super bummed I missed dinner with her. We've been planning this for a month. She drove up here just for this."

Darcie's mouth twisted in commiseration. "That sucks. What about-"

"Do you know where I can find Lena the Lawyer's office?" a young man interrupted. He stood in the doorway holding two big brown bags and looking completely lost. "Guy said it should be around here."

"I'm Lena," I said. "But I'm not a law-"

"Good enough for me," the delivery guy said before I could finish. He dropped the two bags on the desk, nearly knocking Darcie off in the process.

"I didn't order anything," I told him, frowning at the bags. "I don't have any money to pay you."

The delivery guy shrugged. "Guy who ordered it already paid. Tip and everything."

I reached for one of the bags, hoping to find a receipt. There had to be some sort of mistake. The food was probably for the lawyers upstairs. I looked up to ask the delivery guy for more information, but he was already gone.

"He left..." I said, staring at the empty door and then at the bags.

"Well, open it." Darcie grabbed one of the bags, pulled it open, and started pulling out containers of food. I did the same to the other bag until all the food was laid out on the desk.

"Wow. I hope you're hungry," Darcie murmured. There was meatloaf with mashed potatoes, salmon with some sort of rice, roasted chicken on a bed of noodles, a big bowl of amazing looking salad with three different kinds of dressing on the side, and a huge plate of decadent-looking brownies. It was enough food to feed an army.

"It must be for upstairs..." It smelled so good. My mouth watered and I hated the idea of giving it away and eating a crusty granola bar.

"Well, here's a note..." Darcie informed me, pulling a card out from her food bag. She cleared her throat and began reading. "Dear Lena, congratulations on your case. I hope this is better than pizza. Aiden."

"Aiden?" I grabbed the note from her hand. The note was typed and very clear. "He sent me dinner. *He sent me dinner?*"

"Someone's got an admirer," Darcie sang. I fully expected her to start into "Lena and Aiden sitting in a tree..."

"How hungry did he think I am?" I asked her, looking at all the food. I was having trouble comprehending just how nice it was to have someone send me dinner. He was basically a stranger, but he had listened and cared enough to send me exactly what I needed. I thought I might cry.

"Beef, chicken, fish, and vegetarian," Darcie explained, pointing to each dish. "He was just making sure you got something you liked. I hope you got his number."

I flipped the card over. Other than the fourteen words congratulating me, it was empty. "Nope. I didn't even get his last name. I think he was a client's assistant or something."

"Well, he can assist me anytime he wants," Darcie said with a wink. "If he fed me this well, I don't think Greg would even mind."

I snickered. Greg, Darcie's husband and love of her life, would most certainly mind. Unless Aiden fed him too. Then he might go along with it.

"There's no way I'm going to be able to eat all of this. You want some?" I motioned to all the food.

"I thought you'd never ask," she replied, handing me a plastic fork. "Polite or our usual?"

"Do you even have to ask?" I stabbed my fork into the salmon that was open in front of her. It exploded in my mouth with lemony goodness. She reached over my arm and took a heaping fork-full of mashed potatoes and stuck them in her mouth.

"You have to try these. I'm pretty sure they're made of heaven," Darcie moaned. I loaded up my own fork and tasted them. They were creamy and delicious with a buttery goodness and just a hint of garlic.

"Probably the best potatoes I've ever had. Even better than Mom's," I gushed, reaching for another bite. She knocked my fork away with hers to defend the potatoes from me, but I got a fork in anyway.

"You need to marry this guy," Darcie informed me as she stuffed another bite into her mouth. "Anyone who sends something this delicious has to be a keeper."

"I'll work on that," I said dryly. I didn't even have his last name, let alone a way to marry him. I left the potatoes alone this time and took another bite of the salmon. This was the best meal I'd had in weeks.

"Um, how do I get out of here?" A voice asked, disrupting my salmon and potato bliss. I looked up to see the delivery guy standing in the doorway. The attitude from earlier was replaced with a bashful blush.

I looked over at Darcie as she furiously stuffed potatoes into her mouth. There was no way she was going to leave those potatoes. "Don't eat all of it, okay? I need to drop some stuff off with Calvin, so I'll show him out as I go."

"I make no promises," she managed to say around her mouthful of food.

I laughed as I grabbed the pictures off the printer and put them and the USB drive with all my findings in a folder. With a little bit of luck, I would have these to Calvin and be back to my food in no time.

"This way," I told the delivery guy. Since he wasn't offering to carry my books, I was showing him out first. "They really need to put up a sign down here or something. People keep getting lost down here. This is the third time today."

He followed me silently until he could see the elevators at which point he took off without even saying goodbye.

"Have a great evening!" I called out after him. I wasn't surprised or terribly disappointed when he didn't say anything. Most people around here didn't. Sometimes I wondered if I was invisible or if people really were just that rude.

I groaned as I reached Calvin's office. The light was off. I knocked, and checked the door, but it was locked. Of course, he got to go home while I stayed here working. I hit his number on my phone.

"Hey, Calvin," I said when his voice-mail picked up without even ringing. "I finished that discovery file you wanted, but you're not here. I'll try Alexa."

As much as I didn't want to call her, I knew I would get in trouble later if I didn't at least try. Alexa's phone rang twice before switching to voice-mail. I did my best to keep my irritation under control. Instead I went for passive aggressive. "Hi, Alexa. Calvin had me work on that discovery file for the Preston case you were supposed to do. I have it done. I guess they'll just wait until morning."

I clicked the end-call button and then banged my hand against Calvin's locked door. This was a huge case and I knew the partners would be furious if they found out the two of them had left work undone on it. I had stayed late and missed my dinner reservations for them, yet neither one of them could be bothered to even pick up their phones.

I thought about just sliding the file under his door and going back to my delicious mashed potatoes. Or what was left of them. I even started to lean over to set it on the floor before I thought better of it. If I left the file here, Calvin and Alexa would just take full credit for it in the morning. The pictures were going to keep this lawsuit from trial and save our client millions. I deserved at least a pat on the back for finding them.

I checked the case file header. The partner running the case was Kathryn McDonald. I would just have to bring it up to her office and slide it under her door. That's where it would end up eventually, I was just skipping the step where Calvin got the credit instead of me.

I skipped the elevator and took the stairs up the one floor. Since I didn't have an armload of books, the stairs were faster. The cement was cold on my feet and I regretted my decision almost immediately. But, by taking the stairs I could pretend that my elevated heart rate was from exercise and not from the idea of what was going to happen to me when Calvin found out I had gone over his head.

The light was on in Kathryn's office and the door was open. I wasn't expecting that. I had thoroughly planned on just sliding the file under the door and scurrying away. My name was on the files, but I certainly wasn't ready to go in front of one of the nation's leading lawyers. The woman sitting at that desk was one of my personal heroes. I was terrified that she would find my work wanting.

I stood for a moment of indecision until I remembered Aiden saying he didn't think I'd be a lower level employee for long. I had gold-plated information. I had everything to gain from giving it to her and nothing to lose. If a stranger who had known me for five minutes thought I could be something, then I had no reason not to at least hand the file to her.

I knocked on the open door, buoyed by Aiden's words before I could talk myself out of it. "Ms. McDonald?"

An imposing woman looked up from her desk. Her blonde hair was graying, but instead of making her look old, it made her look distinguished. She had her glasses perched on the tip of her nose as she read over a document in her hand. She was exactly what I thought a lawyer should look like and everything I wanted to become.

"Yes?" Kathryn McDonald responded, sounding slightly annoyed at the intrusion. A hot sweat spread out on my stomach and the palms of my hands. Maybe I should have just left the file for Calvin.

"Ms. McDonald, I'm Lena Masterson- a paralegal downstairs..." I fumbled with my words. I had no idea what I was doing up here, let alone talking to the head partner of the firm.

"And?" Ms. McDonald blinked slowly at me, waiting for me to stop talking gibberish.

"I'm sorry to bother you- I just came across, I mean I found..." I stopped and took a deep breath, trying to center myself. Aiden had thought I could do this. I began again. "I found some information that will win you the Preston case."

"A bold claim," Ms. McDonald said as she set her reading down. I had her complete attention now and I started to shake. "Let me see it."

I nearly tripped as I hurried over to her desk to hand her the file. "I printed the relevant pictures, but the original screen shots are on the USB as well as the-"

"Where did you find these?" Ms. McDonald cut me off.

"On the myFace pages of the plaintiff's friends. He was smart enough to un-tag himself so they didn't show up on his personal page, but several of his friends have all their pictures set to public view. I recognized him as soon as I saw them." I swallowed hard. I had been expecting her to smile, but so far she was just watching me with a perfect, unemotional lawyer mask.

"Why didn't the attorney I had assigned to this find these?" she asked, holding up a file from her desk. I recognized it as the file I had delivered to Calvin earlier in the day from Alexa.

"I'm not sure, ma'am," I said quietly. Ms. McDonald's sharp green eyes flashed up at me. She didn't believe me. She tossed Alexa's thin file down on her desk and picked mine up again, evaluating the contents.

"Why didn't you bring this to Calvin? I don't usually have paralegals bringing me their findings directly." She turned a page and looked it over. I really hoped I hadn't missed any spelling errors.

"He isn't here and he didn't answer his phone," I said carefully. I didn't want to get him in trouble, but Kathryn McDonald deserved to know the truth. Her eyebrows raised slightly and displeasure flickered across her green eyes. Calvin was going to have a bad day tomorrow. "I thought the discovery was important enough that it should get to you tonight. Before you meet with the clients in the morning."

"You're LTM5?" she asked, pointing to my initials at the bottom of the page. The computer automatically printed the user's initials on everything. It made figuring out who had done what research more effective and the billing department could then bill appropriately.

"Yes, ma'am." I nodded, doing my best not to nervously fidget. I realized I was bare foot in her office.

"I see your initials on most of my cases. I thought for sure you were an attorney." Ms. McDonald set my file down on the desk in front of her and smiled at me. She went from scary intimidating to attractive when she smiled. "Thank you, Lena. This is excellent work. You were right to bring it to me."

I let out a nervous breath I hadn't realized I was holding. "Thank you, ma'am."

Ms. McDonald looked up at me and gave a short nod

before turning back to her original reading. I stood there for a moment before I realized that I had been dismissed. As quickly as I could without tripping over my feet, I hurried out of the office.

My heart was fluttering as I stepped into the elevator and pressed the button to go down. Once the doors closed, I started to laugh. It was more of just a release of nerves than actually finding the situation funny, but it still felt good. I leaned against the wall, giggling as I tried to figure out if today had been good or bad. I didn't get my raise and I had to stay late and miss dinner with my sister, but in exchange, the big boss had complimented me and I had gotten a handsome man to carry my books and buy me dinner. Just thinking about him made me smile.

*Good day* I decided, stepping into the spot I had stood earlier in with Aiden. Aiden had made it a very good day.

## CHAPTER 5

The Chicago sky was a steel gray that threatened to bring rain or snow later in the day. A cold wind whistled between the buildings and whipped at my hair with angry fingers. I pulled my coat tighter and sipped my coffee as I hurried into the lobby of the skyscraper that housed the McDonald, Smith and Ward offices.

The lobby hummed with conversations as people piled into elevators on their way to work or waited for coworkers under the lofty marble columns. Darcie waved as soon as she saw me, hurrying across the lobby to join me. Since she had helped me put my leftovers in the fridge, I had a sneaky suspicion she would be joining me for lunch and eating most of it.

"You get that guy's number yet?" Darcie asked, bumping my shoulder with hers in friendly greeting.

"I wish," I said, taking another sip of coffee. My coffee pot was still broken, so I was enjoying a latte from the coffee shop on my way. "I'm not one hundred percent certain he wasn't just a figment of my stressed out imagination."

"Oh, he was real all right," Darcie assured me. "And so

were those potatoes last night. I think they must have used real cream to get them so good."

I laughed, shaking my head. Books and food were that girl's passions. Together we stood in line to get on the elevator up to our respective floors. "I'm fairly sure they put crack cocaine in them to make them that good—oof!"

A man in a black leather jacket ran smack into my shoulder, knocking me off balance and spilling coffee down my arm and across his sleeve.

"Hey! Watch where you're going!" the guy snarled, turning to stare me down. He was bigger than I was with mean features and cold eyes.

"I'm so sorry..." I stammered. "I didn't mean to..."

"Damn right you didn't," he growled, getting into my face. "Do you know how much this jacket cost?"

I looked down at his jacket to see the last of my coffee running off it. My own arm was soaked with latte and I was just glad that it had cooled enough that it didn't hurt. I had no idea how I was going to fix this. I shrunk back, unable to meet his angry gaze. "I'm so sorry..."

The man puffed up his chest. People were starting to stop and watch. I had the sick feeling in my stomach that I was about to get pummeled.

"You ran into her, jackass," Darcie interjected, stepping into the shrinking space between the man and me. She had her "touch me and die" face on. "I suggest you keep walking."

The man looked her up and down once before deciding that she really would cut him if he tried anything. Darcie wasn't big enough to be intimidating, but she made an angry cobra look like a kitten when she was mad. He took a step back and rolled his shoulders before walking away like that was his plan all along.

"Thanks," I said quietly as I pulled my coffee-soaked jacket off and hung it over my arm.

"The guy was a jerk," Darcie said, flipping her blonde hair back over her shoulder. "You okay?"

"It's just coffee. It'll come out in the wash. At least it wasn't hot. I really should watch where I'm going." I shrugged.

Darcie gave an exasperated sigh and put her hands on my shoulders. "Lena, you know I love you, right?" She waited a moment for me to nod before continuing. "That wasn't even close to being your fault. You can't let people walk all over you like that. You got to stand up for yourself. You are worth standing up for."

"I'll work on it," I promised, not meeting her eyes and instead peering into my now empty coffee cup.

"You're going to do a lot more than just work on it." Darcie was getting her fighting face on again. "I'm serious as a heart attack. You don't take shit from anyone. Not even me."

"How am I supposed to do that, Darcie?" I asked, meeting her flashing eyes. "If I don't take your shit, I won't have anyone to take mine."

"Smart ass." Darcie narrowed her eyes and evaluated me. "I'm serious, though. I'm going to sign you up for some self-defense classes or something. There's nothing like kicking a man in the balls to make you feel powerful."

The two men standing nearest to us both skittered in opposite directions.

"Sure, Darcie," I conceded, but I knew she was right. I let Alexa walk all over me. I didn't defend myself to Calvin during my review, or tell him no when he had me stay late. I was surprised that I had even spoken to Kathryn last night, and the only reason I had done that was because I was thinking of Aiden.

I tossed the empty cup into the trash and stepped onto the elevator with Darcie. We moved toward the back with surprising ease. Apparently talking about ball kicking made people give us space.

"Did you ever hear anything from Calvin or Alexa last night?" Darcie stepped closer to me to allow more passengers on the elevator. "You said you called them before you saw Kathryn."

I shook my head. "Nope. But I'm looking forward to the fallout today. There's no way they won't at least get reprimanded for leaving early. Am I a bad person for hoping they get publicly shamed?

"Nope. Those two have screwed you more ways than I care to count. It's time they had to take responsibility for using you the way they do." Darcie leaned against the elevator wall as we started our upward descent. "Oh, hey – did you hear that Smith got the big murder case?"

"What big murder case?" I asked, confused. Elijah Smith was one of the founding partners of the firm and was considered one of the best criminal defense lawyers in the nation, but I hadn't heard of any potential cases.

"The sports star from Texas – the one that probably killed his wife – hired Smith to defend him," Darcie replied.

"I thought that he already had that lawyer from Washington. Isn't that case like, two weeks from trial? They switched council this late?" I frowned, trying to figure it out. My mind was already going through all the paperwork and legal issues with switching representation this close to a trial.

"Yup. Don't you watch the news? There was a huge scandal with the previous firm," Darcie informed me.

"Because I have *so* much time to watch TV," I replied sarcastically. "Wait – you said it was Smith?"

"Yeah. Smith." Darcie nodded. I wanted to whoop and dance for joy, but the elevator was still too crowded.

"I'm going to get to go to trial with him. I'll be in the courtroom for this!" I had to whisper or I knew I would scream it out. I couldn't believe my luck.

"Get out! How?" Darcie asked, an excited smile filling her face.

"It's part of the "Grooming the Next Generation of Lawyers" thing that the partners put on every year. Smith picks a non-lawyer employee who wants to pursue a law degree and shows them just how high they can go," I explained. "I was selected as the employee this year, but the Ohio case was pretty much over, so I was promised his next big case. This is the next case!"

"That's freaking fantastic!" Darcie hugged me, but pulled back after a moment with worry on her face. "But aren't Calvin and Alexa going to try and block you from doing it?"

"They can't. This is through the partners. I have a letter from Smith himself saying I get to participate on his next case." The odds of them going against the partners were so slim that I laughed, almost giddy with excitement. "This is over their heads as a mandate from their bosses. They can't stop me!"

Darcie pulled me into another hug, squeezing me tight enough to make it hard to breathe. "Congrats, Lena! You deserve it so much!"

"Thanks. I'll just be doing coffee runs and observing, but," I grinned, feeling my dreams coming true, "I'm going to learn so much. It's perfect."

"I'm proud of you," Darcie told me. The elevator chimed my floor. " See you for lunch?"

"Definitely," I answered, stepping off on the fifteenth floor. Darcie waved as the elevator doors closed and took her up to the sixteenth floor. Someday, I would be going up there instead of down here to the Dungeons.

The office was the usual buzz of morning business, but it sounded happier to me today than it had in a long time. Even my little work station looked better today and I didn't even frown at the stack of papers already waiting for my attention. In two weeks, I'd be in Texas helping Smith with the legal case of a lifetime. If that on my resume didn't get me a spot at Harvard, I'd eat my shoe. Plus, the icing on the cake was that I would be away from Alexa and Calvin.

"I heard about your little stunt last night," Alexa informed me, gliding up to my desk. I wondered how someone so pretty could be so evil. She was tall with dark, glossy hair that was always perfectly coiffed. Her eyes were a unique shade of gray with lashes so long they made a breeze when she blinked. Add in perfect porcelain skin, legs that stretched into infinity and a waist that was built for the designer skirts she always seemed to wear, and she was gorgeous. Gorgeous and incredibly evil.

"I'm not sure what you mean, Alexa," I replied diplomatically as I sat down at my desk. Most people thought that because she was so pretty there was no way she could be smart. I had learned the hard way that she had a ruthless mind that was always two steps ahead of everyone else. Alexa always got what she wanted. Always.

"Don't play coy, Lena. It doesn't become you," she sneered. "You went to the partners behind my back. You went to Kathryn without consulting me or even Calvin. The whole upstairs is talking about how the paralegal went straight to Kathryn on the Preston case. You breached protocol and there are some very unhappy people up there."

"Are they talking about what I found?" I asked, shuffling the papers on my desk. The last thing I had been expecting today was to get in trouble. Since Alexa was involved, I should have known it would happen. That was just the way my luck at work was tending to go this week.

Alexa ignored my question and instead leaned over my desk and pitched her voice so anyone nearby could hear. "You report to me. I'm a lawyer and you're a paralegal. There's a reason why I make four times your salary. You had no right to bother Kathryn with something so trivial. Especially just to spite me because of your bad review."

A secretary stopped dead in her tracks and stared. Heads popped up over dividers. Everyone was tuning in to watch me get the scolding of a lifetime. My stomach was turning to acid.

"You mean bringing her the pictures I found on myFace?" I asked, struggling to keep my voice steady. She had just announced my bad review to the entire office. I set my jacket on my desk and the card from Aiden's dinner fluttered out from the pocket.

"Yes, the pictures from myFace," she repeated, her voice dripping with derision as I picked up the card and set it on my desk. "That was my case, Lena. *Mine.* You were supposed to go through me and I'm going to make sure the partners know you went over my head. I walked in this morning expecting a report from you only to find out you went straight to Kathryn. I'm going to be bringing up your insubordination with her. I know you don't like how I work, but that is unacceptable behavior."

I stared at her for a moment, unbelieving at how clueless she was. The acid in my stomach was changing to triumph.

She had no idea how much trouble she was in. She just thought that I was out to get her as much as she was out to get me, and thought I would use her tactics. She had no idea what I had found or how poorly it reflected on her.

*You are worth standing up for.* Darcie was right. I was going places and I could stand up for myself. I was worth more than Alexa or Calvin realized. *You won't be low level for long...* Aiden's words echoed in my mind, mingling with Darcie's. If someone like him thought I was going places, then someone like Alexa had no right to challenge me.

"You mean the pictures from myFace?" I repeated, drawing courage from the card. I was worth something. "The ones *you* should have gotten in the first place? The ones that were part of the job you tried to pawn off on me and when I said no, you did a half-ass job on?"

Alexa's mouth opened to contradict me, but I kept going. Now that I had started, there was no way for me to stop. "Then, when I had to go back and do your job for you- and actually did it- I found the case saving photos? The ones that are going to keep it from going to trial and will save our client millions. *Those* myFace pictures?"

I paused for a moment to catch my breath. The crowd that was pretending not to watch us murmured. I knew I was playing with fire, but if felt good to be the one with the matches for once. "But you know, maybe you mean the ones that I tried to give to Calvin or you last night. Except neither one of you was in the office or answering your phones. But at least Kathryn was here, you know, working after hours on *your* case. Are those the ones we're talking about?"

Alexa's eyes darkened and her mouth condensed into a thin, ugly line. She looked over at the secretary that was now snickering in the hallway. The girl yelped and took off like she'd been burned by Alexa's gaze. The rest of the employees scattered like fallen marbles. Served her right for picking the time when the most people would be present to try and corner me.

"You think you're so smart," she murmured. The darkness on her face twisted into a merciless, confident smile. "Enjoy this feeling, Ms. Masterson, because I'm going to destroy you. When I'm done with you, you're going to wish you had never even heard the word 'lawyer'."

I put on my best polite smile. It was a struggle not to shout, "You only have two weeks to do it!" but I kept quiet. Instead, I just replied, "Have a great rest of your day, Ms. Jones."

Alexa's smile dropped and she turned on her heel to stalk off back to her office. I didn't move until she was gone. I was shaking too much.

I let out a long breath when her office door slammed shut. I couldn't believe I had just done that. I had a feeling it was going to bite me in the ass eventually, but for now, it felt good. Besides, in two weeks, I would be out of her reach. She had no way of knowing that I was set to go to Texas with Smith. The decision had happened before she arrived here. With any luck, I'd be gone before she could do anything about it.

I looked down at my stack of papers, trying to get ready to work, but I couldn't concentrate. I kept daydreaming about going to Texas and showing everyone how useful I really was. Maybe I'd even figure out the argument that would win Smith the case. I'd have the scholarship and a guaranteed job when I graduated.

I picked up the card from Aiden. He'd be impressed too. He'd find me at the trial and tell me just how impressed and proud of me he was. How he knew I could do it. He'd even kiss me. We'd get married, I'd be a famous lawyer, and we'd both live happily ever after. It was perfect.

"Lena," a voice called, bringing back to earth. I started and opened my eyes to see one of the legal assistants staring at me like I was crazy. I wondered just how long she'd been there watching me daydream. "Mr. Smith would like to meet you upstairs in his office."

I grinned. This was it. I was on my way. "Thank you. I'll be right up."

The assistant shrugged and hurried off. I smoothed my hair and made sure my shirt was straight. This was going to be good. I tucked the card gently back into my coat pocket to keep it safe. The only thing that could make this day better would be a visit from Aiden. A girl could dream.

## CHAPTER 6

*I* couldn't keep the grin off my face as I hurried upstairs. Darcie gave me a big thumbs up as I passed the library on my way to Smith's office. I could hardly wait to get in there, but I made sure to walk calmly and professionally, even though I really just wanted to do cartwheels in the hallway.

Mr. Smith's secretary sat at a large desk guarding the entrance to his office. It looked as though a paper avalanche had hit her desk overnight as she sorted and organized the files that must be about the new case. I cleared my throat and she looked up from her work, her face betraying nothing.

"Go on in," she told me. "They're expecting you."

I grinned at her her, but she just returned to her piles of paper. I was excited and nervous and fairly sure that I might vibrate off the floor with all the emotions running through me. I opened his office door, stepped inside, and immediately stopped smiling. The happy vibrations were gone. I wasn't floating. I was sinking.

Sitting perched on the edge of Smith's desk was Alexa.

Calvin sat in a chair beside her while Smith himself stood. I couldn't think of a single good reason why the two of them would be in here. I wished I hadn't left the card in my jacket pocket. I needed a little courage.

"Lena. Good, you're here," Smith greeted me. He was an older gentleman, probably in his mid-sixties, though his actual age was a closely guarded secret. His hair was thick and gray, but his brown eyes were quick and sharp. "Now we can get started."

I looked nervously from face to face, trying to figure out what exactly was going on. I swallowed hard as the door shut behind me. I didn't move away; I needed to know I had an exit if things went as bad as I was afraid of.

"Now, I'm aware that you were selected as the employee for the "Grooming the Next Generation" program this year. I remember picking you myself," Smith started. All three of them were staring at me. I felt like a specimen in an experiment. Any moment, one of them was going to do something terrible to see how I would respond.

"Yes, sir," I responded meekly.

"As such, you are supposed to come with me on my next case. I don't know if you watched the news this morning, but I was just hired on the Stephan Myers case in Texas." He waited for me to nod.

"I had heard that, sir." I held my breath, waiting for him to tell me that I was going in front of Alexa and Calvin. This could still turn out okay.

Smith's shoulders dropped a little his brows came together as he looked down, as if summoning the courage to continue. I had seen him do this in the courtroom for the jury. He had bad news for me. "I'm afraid I won't be bringing you."

"What?" I gasped, feeling the air rush from the room. "Why?"

Smith took a step toward me, holding his hands out apologetically. "It was brought to my attention that Alexa here has never been on a big case like this before, but that she has a real interest in them." He put his hand on my shoulder, as if he were trying to comfort me.

I was certain I was about to be physically ill. "I still don't understand why I can't go..."

Smith smiled sadly and squeezed my shoulder. "There are a limited amount of spots on the team. I need lawyers more than I need paralegals. I'm sorry."

Alexa and Calvin smiled like jackals as I my dreams evaporated.

"But, I had a letter from you..." I said softly. This couldn't be happening. It wasn't possible.

"I know." Smith sighed and let go of my shoulder. "But given your recent evaluation, I need to bring people I can trust to get the job done."

I tasted bile as I threw up in my mouth a little.

"I see," I said slowly. Though, really, I didn't. I didn't see how a good-for-nothing, brand new lawyer with absolutely no trial experience got to go on an all-expenses paid trip to watch one of the best criminal defense lawyers in the country work while the paralegal that had been promised, and actually could help, had to stay home. I didn't understand it at all.

"I know this is a disappointment, Lena," Smith said slowly. I hated that he used my first name like he knew me. He didn't know me because if he did, he wouldn't have done this. "There will be other cases. Ones closer to home and more your speed."

My eyes nearly bugged out of my head. Alexa smirked. I

wanted to scream, to tell Smith exactly what kind of lawyer he was getting with Alexa, but nothing would come out. I stayed quiet. I stayed small and insignificant.

"I wanted to tell you in person," Smith concluded. He stepped away from me and back toward Alexa and Calvin and folded his hands behind his back like he did at the end of a presentation to the jury. "Now if you'll excuse us, I need to get everyone who is coming to Houston with me together. Would you mind letting my secretary know she can send in the others on your way out?"

"Of course, sir," I replied meekly, turning blindly to reach for the door. I couldn't get out of the room fast enough.

As soon as the secretary saw me emerge, she nodded to the newly gathered crowd to go in. A stream of lawyers poured past me, and not a single one said a word.

"I told you not to mess with me," Alexa said, coming to the door. She smiled, her teeth cruel and bright. "Have fun staying here. I'll send you a postcard."

She slammed the door shut behind her. Through it, I heard Smith's voice followed by a cheer from the lawyers. Tears filled my vision and I stumbled away from what should have been mine.

## CHAPTER 7

*I* didn't want to see Darcie yet, but I didn't know where else to go. The library was the one place that I could escape to; I could hide in a book better than I could hide behind my very open desk. I managed to keep myself contained until I stepped through the big glass doors protecting the books before I lost it.

Mercifully, the library was empty. Darcie must have had to deliver something. The placard on her desk said she'd be back in fifteen minutes, but I was just glad to have a the library to myself for a moment. As much as I loved my friend, I wasn't ready to tell anyone how crushed I was. Alexa had beaten me. She had destroyed me and I hadn't seen it coming.

I went to my favorite desk in the library. It was tucked up against a window and hidden from the rest of the library by bookshelves. I'd never seen anyone else use it, since most people preferred the big tables close to the entrance to work. It was my secret place in the office where I could read and research without anyone bothering me. Today, I had no plans for research. I just needed a place to hide.

I sat down on the comfy office chair, pulling my knees up into my chest. The tears started falling, silently tracing paths down my cheeks. For a few glorious hours, I had thought I was going places. I thought I was going to observe a high-profile murder case. My acceptance to Harvard was practically assured. The scholarship was in my pocket.

Now it was all just sand on the wind. Painful and messy.

I couldn't believe Smith picked Alexa over me. She was the last person that should be going to Texas. She could barely remember what a jury was called, let alone be in the same room as one. He probably picked her because she would look good on camera. She was tall and beautiful, especially when compared to a short, little paralegal with too much excitement in her eyes.

I wiped my cheek with the palm of my hand, trying to wipe away the sadness and bitterness with the tears. I hoped Alexa showed Smith her true colors. The idea of her ruining the entire murder case with her ineptness was appealing, except for the part that it wouldn't be Alexa's name that was ruined. It would be Smith's. He was an excellent attorney and I didn't want to see Alexa take someone of his skill down because she was an idiot.

The unfairness ached like an open wound. I had worked so hard. I deserved this chance. Even though murder trials weren't where my legal interests lay, I had been excited. It would have been the experience of a lifetime. Instead I was just going to stay in Chicago and pray that I had enough on my resume to get into a good law school, let alone have a shot at Harvard.

I took a deep shaky breath. At least I wouldn't have to deal with Alexa and Calvin while they were at the trial. My life would certainly be easier without having to be their step-n-fetch-it. I might actually go home on time without them here.

Except I didn't want to go home. The law firm, the courthouse-- they were more my home than my apartment. I was made for the legal world. I ached with betrayal and loss. Everything I wanted in life was crumbling apart and I didn't even have a basket to put the pieces in.

I wiped another set of tears from my cheeks and hugged my knees in tighter. *This isn't the end of the world, it just feels like it.* My Mom used to tell me that all the time when I was a kid. *This too shall pass.* I knew it was true, but for now, I just wished it didn't hurt so much.

"I DIDN'T KNOW anyone else knew about this spot."

I looked up from my secret desk in the library in surprise. The late afternoon sun reflected warmth across Kathryn McDonald's stern features. She had a large ceramic mug and a legal pad in her hands.

"Ms. McDonald," I stuttered, quickly gathering my things and closing my laptop. "Let me get out of your way."

She waved a hand through the air to negate me. "No, no, don't get up. You were here first." She smiled and pulled a chair over with her free hand. I sat back down, suddenly nervous. "Actually, I was looking for you."

I had already been told by one partner that my dreams were gone. I wasn't looking forward to round two. I was probably going to be fired. Why else would Kathryn McDonald be looking for me?

"I'm sorry I wasn't at my desk." I just needed a chance to explain myself. Maybe I could still manage to keep my job. I didn't have the current "Grooming the Future Generation" option anymore, but I wasn't ready to leave the firm either. "I just couldn't concentrate down there, so I brought my work up here, and-"

"It's a good place to work," Ms. McDonald agreed, cutting off my nervous babble. She set her legal pad down on the edge of the desk and took a sip of tea. She frowned down at it and blew on the steam. It must have been too hot.

"Ms. McDonald, I'm sorry if I bothered you last night. I shouldn't have gone over the associates' heads like that, but I thought you should have the information and--"

"Lena," Ms. McDonald said gently, cutting me off again. She placed one of her hands on mine. "You're not in trouble."

"I'm not?" Relief flooded through me and I no longer thought I might have a heart attack.

"No." Kathryn smiled and shook her head. "Quite the opposite, in fact. I'd like to offer you a job."

I stared at her, utterly confused. "I already have a job... unless I was fired and didn't realize it."

She laughed gently. It was a pleasant, normal sound I wasn't expecting. "I guess it's more of a promotion than a job," she explained, sounding a little unsure of herself. In my head, Kathryn McDonald was a mythic lawyer of epic proportions. I had forgotten that she was human, but sitting here with her, I was slowly changing my opinion. "I'd like you to be my personal paralegal."

"What?" I started to shake my head no. There was no way I was qualified to be a personal anything for a lawyer as good as Kathryn. "You have plenty of associates and more qualified--"

"Lena," she cut me off again. The quirk of her mouth at least suggested she was finding my babbling amusing rather than irritating. "Most of the files I get from the associates have your initials on them. I've seen your work. You do as well, if not better, than several associates I know. You may not have the letters after your name, but you have experience and I'd rather have someone with experience and a brain helping me than fancy letters."

I sat there, in the presence of my legal hero, completely shocked. My ability to speak completely vanished. She was offering me a dream job as well as giving me the best compliment I could ask for. I couldn't find the words. Kathryn sipped on her tea again, this time finding it the right temperature.

"Did you know I was a paralegal?" she asked, conversationally. I was fairly sure I had to be dreaming. I shook my head no and she continued. "I was. I became a paralegal because someone said I would be good at it. I became a lawyer because I knew I would be fantastic at it."

I was still a little in shock as she sipped her tea again. She watched me, her green eyes taking in every detail and analyzing it. I hoped I didn't look like a disappointment.

"I tell you this because you remind me a lot of myself." Kathryn set her cup down on the desk. "I've been searching for someone since my previous paralegal retired. She was good, but you're better. What I need is another me and you're the next best thing."

"So you want me to be your personal paralegal?" I asked, sounding like a very confused parrot. I was still trying to get over the fact that she was just sitting here telling me her life story like a normal person. This was beyond what I thought could happen today.

"Yes. I want you to work solely on my cases. You report to me and only me. You will attend all court hearings with me and accompany me on meetings." She picked her cup back up and took another sip. It smelled like some sort of green tea. "You will work closely with my secretary and the associates under me. It will be long hours, there will be travel, and I expect perfection."

"All court hearings?" I whispered. Just seeing her once in court would be amazing, let alone getting to go to all of them.

"Yes." She frowned over her tea cup, thinking that I was going to object. "Is that a problem?"

"No!" I managed to choke out. That was the opposite of a problem. It was a dream come true. "It's fantastic! I've got to be dreaming. This is too good to be real..."

Kathryn grinned, obviously enjoying this. "It gets better."

"Better?"

"You get a raise. A good one. Better than good, really." She sipped nonchalantly on her tea as she slid a piece of paper with an absurdly high number on it across the desk.

I couldn't find the words for the millionth time that day. Instead, my mouth just hung open in disbelief.

"There is one downside, though," Kathryn informed me. She lowered her cup to her lap. "You would be ineligible for the Grooming the Future Mentor Observation with Elijah Smith. You can't observe his cases if you're busy with mine."

"I'm all right with that! I'd be observing you instead," I gasped. My heart was singing hymns. This had to be a dream.

"You'd be doing more than just observing. You'll be working. You want the job?" Kathryn asked. Her voice was controlled, but her eyes sparkled with the joy of offering someone their dreams.

"Yes!" I practically shouted. "Yes, I want the job!"

She grinned. "Excellent. Hand off your current workload

to someone else and clean out your desk. My secretary will show you your new workspace next to my office."

I was moving up the the sixteenth floor. I was going to be in court with Kathryn McDonald. For that, I would have taken a pay cut, but instead I was getting a pay raise. I couldn't wipe the smile off my face. I wanted to pinch myself, but I didn't dare. I didn't want to wake up from this. "Yes, ma'am. I'll tell Mr. Smith about dropping the mentor program on my way."

"No need," she informed me as she stood and put her chair away. "I told Elijah to pick someone else for your spot last night."

"But you just asked..."

Kathryn laughed and her green eyes shone with cleverness. "I already knew you were going to take the position. I was counting on it. This was just to make sure you knew where to look for your new desk."

ONE HOUR later I stepped into Kathryn's office, ready to start my new job. I was all moved in to my new office space just outside of Kathryn's corner suite. Even the desk was bigger and better than anything we had down stairs. Alexa's desk was just plywood with a nice paint job-- this desk was solid wood the whole way through with the McDonald, Smith and Ward MSW logo on the front. I kept expecting a camera crew to jump out at any moment and tell me it was all just a big prank.

"All settled?" Kathryn asked coming around to greet me. "What do you think?"

"That you're going to realize I'm just a paralegal and send me back," I answered honestly.

Kathryn evaluated me with keen eyes. "Do you know how much money and time you saved my clients by finding those pictures? Millions." She motioned to a stack of files nearly ready to fall off her desk. "Every single one of those files has your initials all over them. I know good work when I see it. If you think I would make a mistake as big as hiring an incompetent personal paralegal, then you should leave right now. Go back to The Dungeon."

I stayed put. I wasn't lower level.

"That's what I thought," she murmured as she sat at her desk. "Now, you see that stack of files? I need you to go through them and get me ready for trial."

I swallowed my stomach back down. I could do this. I was ready.

Opening the first file, I smiled. This case was easy. I recognized it as the case I had worked on for Joffrey.

"Yes, ma'am. I'll get right on this." This is what I was made to do.

## CHAPTER 8

After three days of officially working as Kathryn's paralegal, I still felt like I was a very small fish in a very big ocean. I knew almost all her cases from front to back, but the newness of the position and the sudden change from nobody to somebody was messing with my head.

It wasn't that I didn't know what to do, quite the opposite really. Working for Kathryn let me use all the skills I had accumulated the past few years. By the end of my first day, Kathryn was already telling me how pleased she was and how I had accomplished more than she had even hoped I would.

It was just that I had this terrible fear that I would be fired from my dream job at any moment. This was just so wonderful that I couldn't see how I deserved it. It was too perfect. I kept pushing the limits of my skills, expecting to fail like I always did. Yet, Kathryn kept telling me what a wonderful job I was doing and how I was making her life easier.

"You are afraid of success," Darcie told me that morning

on our way up. I loved getting to ride the elevator with her the whole sixteen floors now. "You have got to believe in yourself. Kathryn believes in you, I believe in you, and that piece of paper from cute Book Guy you keep in your pocket believes in you."

"I hate you sometimes," I informed her. I had no idea how she knew about the paper.

"Yeah, well." She shrugged. "Just wait until I sign you up for that ball kicking class. Then you'll love me again."

With that I rolled my eyes and started my third official morning as Kathryn's paralegal. I walked in to her office and she looked up from her writing and frowned. I smoothed my hands down my slacks, suddenly feeling under-dressed and unworthy in her gaze. I knew it had been too good to last.

"We need to get you some new clothes. I can't have you dressing like that in front of clients." That was not what I had been expecting. She picked up her phone and hit a button. I looked down at my clothes. I had on simple black dress pants and a cute polka-dot blouse. I thought it was a very work appropriate outfit.

"I have suits I can wear," I offered. I was determined to make this work. I wanted to keep this job.

"Are they Prada?" Kathryn raised her eyebrows as she waited for the other line to pick up.

"No. JC Penny," I admitted. There was no way I could afford anything close to Prada level suits on my salary. Maybe one or two with my new salary, but definitely not any with the old one.

"I need you to look like you work for me. My clients pay a lot of money to have the best, so I need you to look like the best. Consider it another perk of the job," she explained.

I looked down at the spot where her desk met the floor. I had no way to pay for an expensive suit.

"It goes on the company credit card," Kathryn informed me. "Don't you worry about the money. It counts as a business expense."

I shifted my weight as she focused her attention to the phone conversation. I liked my clothes, but I understood Kathryn's point. It was time to dress to impress. With clients worth billions of dollars, she needed me to look like I belonged among them.

"Claire, schedule a fitting with Raoul this evening for Lena..." she ordered. The person on the other line responded and she frowned before putting her hand over the mouthpiece. "What are you doing right now?"

"Um, whatever you tell me to." I shrugged nervously. "I just finished the last item on the list you gave me"

Kathryn's eyebrows raised in approval. "Excellent. Remind me to give you more tomorrow." She focused back on her phone. "Yes, now will work."

The phone call ended with a click. My palms were sweaty and I was glad I had double checked all my work. If I hadn't, I would have really been freaking out that I had missed something. As it was, I was just partially freaking out. I wanted to be good at this.

Kathryn scribbled something on a piece of paper and handed it to me. "You are to go to this address and do whatever Raoul says to do. He's going to make you look like the McDonald, Smith and Ward employee that you are. Understand?"

I nodded. "Do I need to bring anything?" I was really glad I had chosen to wear my newer underwear this morning.

"Just your smile and my name," Kathryn replied. "Go have fun."

THE ADDRESS WAS one of the Magnificent Mile's fashion boutique. As the company cab pulled up, I nearly called Kathryn to confirm I had the right place. It was the kind of shop that looked so expensive window-shoppers had to pay a fee.

A soft bell chimed on the door as I stepped inside. White walls with artsy black and white photographs hung at strategic intervals throughout the store, but there was a surprising lack of clothing. I picked up a sequined covered dress on a nearby hanger to see a price tag that would pay my rent several times. I nearly dropped the hanger before realizing that would be even worse.

"You must be Kathryn's," a man said, emerging from a back room. He wore simple black pants and a black shirt that hugged his thin frame with a bright blue scarf around his neck.

"That's me," I replied with a laugh. The man grinned, his teeth white against his dark skin. He came closer and I realized he had the most amazing blue eyes. "I don't really know what I'm doing here."

"Well, the clothes out here aren't really for you." He motioned to the sequined dress. "I doubt Kathryn would appreciate that in her office."

I giggled at the image of me sparkling while preparing her legal documents. "No, probably not."

He held out a friendly hand. "I'm Raoul."

"Lena," I replied, taking his hand. His fingers were calloused and his grip strong.

"Come with me, Lena." He grinned. "I'm going to make you look like a star."

THREE HOURS LATER, I had tried on more clothing than I had ever even owned in my entire life. I was exhausted. I had no idea how just putting on and taking off clothes could take so much energy. Suddenly, I could see how the socialites of the world stayed so skinny. All they did was change their clothes.

The door leading to freedom opened and Kathryn walked in. "How's it going, Raoul?"

"Fantastic. I think we have a good base," he answered, handing her his bill.

"A good base?" I repeated quietly, looking at the pile of clothes I had tried on. It was a mountain, yet all I had to show for my work was three suits, two dresses, some dress shirts, four pairs of shoes and the appointment card for another fitting. Apparently, despite trying on fourteen sets of suits that I thought looked great, Raoul felt I needed to get some custom made. I was due to come back for round two in a couple of days.

Kathryn signed the bill for my clothing without even looking at it. I had a feeling I didn't want to know how much it was for. If I did, I wouldn't dare breathe in any of it for fear of ripping a ten thousand dollar stitch.

"Lena," Kathryn asked suddenly. "Do you have a swimsuit?"

"Uh- swimsuit?" I imagined myself walking through the halls of the office in a skimpy bikini. I couldn't imagine why I would need a swimsuit for this job. I was fairly sure that Kathryn was in to men.

"I have some in stock," Raoul said helpfully. "It's off season, but everything is at this time of year."

"Go ahead and bring it out," Kathryn told him. "Can't have her wearing a three-thousand dollar suit to the meetings and a ten dollar bathing suit to the beach."

"Bathing suit?" I asked once Raoul disappeared into his storage room. Kathryn sat down on the couch next to me. "Beach?"

"You are accompanying me to the Travel, Inc. legal meeting," she informed me matter-of-factly.

"What's that and why does it require a swim suit?" I was still confused, but at least it wasn't for the office.

She reached for her briefcase and began looking for something. "Our firm heads all legal council for Travel, Inc. Every year, Travel, Inc. and MSW meet to discuss the future."

"In swimsuits?" I had the sudden image of an entire board room full of high powered business executives in swimsuits. There was a towel on the center of the table and everyone was drinking fruity drinks.

Kathryn must have imagined something similar because she laughed. "The meeting is held at a resort on Key Island." When I showed no recognition of the name, she added, "in the Caribbean."

"Oh." I raised my eyebrows as understanding hit me. "We're going to the Caribbean?"

"I told you this job had travel," Kathryn said, still rooting around in her briefcase for something. "I believe my exact words were, 'It will be long hours, there will be travel, and I expect perfection.'"

"I was thinking travel like to Toledo. The Caribbean sounds great," I said, trying to sound calm and mostly succeeding. This job just kept getting better and better. "You said it was a legal meeting for Travel, Inc.?"

"Yes," she responded. She handed me the file she had been searching for. If I was going to be her personal paralegal, I was going to have to help her manage her files better. "We're the lead firm and will head the meetings."

I flipped through the folder. "I'm afraid I don't know much about Travel, Inc. other than their commercials," I admitted. The file in front of me said they were the world's largest travel website and had recently added a "concierge travel" service that was destroying the competition by leaps and bounds. "Do they not have their own legal department? I would think a billion dollar company would have their own lawyers."

"They do. In addition to their in-house lawyers, they contract out to 15 firms to handle all their legal work," Kathryn explained. "This meeting is where the partners of these firms and the key players for Travel, Inc. meet to make sure we're all on the same page."

"In the Caribbean." I grinned. Screw Texas, I was going to a tropical island instead!

"At a beautiful, all-inclusive resort in the Caribbean," Kathryn amended. She grinned.

"What do you need me to do?" I was already excited. We'd probably be stuck in meetings all day and barely get to see the beach, but I didn't care. I was going to the Caribbean.

"Make me look good. Everything's already prepared, but I need you to make sure I make it to meetings on time, have my presentations up and running, and to help wrangle some of the other firms." She shrugged and leaned back in her chair. "It should actually be a pretty low-key event. Almost vacation-like, really."

"I can do that. When do we leave?" I hadn't taken a vacation in a very long time. I hadn't seen the ocean since I was a kid and we went to Florida for a family trip in high school. I remembered I really liked the water, even though it had been nearly brown with sand.

"Two weeks. We'll be there for six days." She looked at me as if I might complain. My roommate would be able to handle my one little sad plant for six days.

"Consider me already packed," I told her with a grin.

"Just about." Kathryn nodded to the changing room. Right then Raoul returned with a clothing rack full of swimsuits ranging from skimpy bikinis to full pieces my grandmother would be comfortable in.

I took a deep breath and prepared for another round of clothing with Raoul. I wasn't terribly excited about trying on swimsuits, in fact it was something I usually dreaded, but I knew that at the end of it, I would be going to the Caribbean.

I would happily try on swimsuits for that.

## CHAPTER 9

$\mathcal{I}$ stared out the glass doors of my room in awe. Outside the ocean sparkled in blue jewel tones against pristine white sand, rolling and dancing together like lovers. Even through the glass, I could hear the song of the sea, calling me like a siren's song. The bright blue sky stretched out into infinity. It was possibly the most beautiful thing I had ever seen in my life.

I looked down at the schedule in my hand. I was going to get some good time in with that perfect turquoise water. The schedule looked more like a vacation than a conference. There was barely a meeting a day and never for more than a couple of hours. Most of the items on the schedule were for fun events like wine tastings and dancing. Alexa and Calvin could suck it in Texas while I vacationed with Kathryn in the Caribbean. I sent Alexa a silent thank you for taking my spot. She was going on thankless coffee runs while I sunbathed.

It wasn't just the vacation that was making me happy. It was my job. In just two weeks, I had done more with Kathryn than I had ever done with Calvin. Kathryn trusted me and appreciated my ideas and experience. Even though I wasn't a lawyer, she listened to me like I was. For the first time in months, I was appreciated and being used to my full potential.

The only thing that could have made the last two weeks better was if Aiden had come back. I kept my eyes open for him, but I hadn't seen him in the office since that night. When I'd asked around, no one knew who Aiden the Assistant belonged to or where I could find him. If I hadn't kept the note from dinner, I would have thought I had dreamed him up.

A knock on the door interrupted my thoughts. It came from the adjoining door to Kathryn's suite. If I thought my room was luxurious with the ocean view and king sized bed, Kathryn's made it clear that my room was meant for the hired help. She had a huge living room and a giant bedroom that dwarfed even my apartment at home. I had only heard of luxury like this.

"Lena, I'm going to go meet some of the other lawyers for drinks," she informed me. She was wearing a low cut sundress that showed off just how fit she had stayed through the years. Her hair was down and she almost looked relaxed. It was a far departure from the perfect lawyer I had worked with for the past two weeks, but I liked it. "The evening is all yours. I'll see you tomorrow for the first official meeting."

"I'll make sure everything is ready, Ms. McDonald. Have a wonderful evening." I grinned at her.

"We're not in front of clients here. We'll be with colleagues pretty much this whole trip, so you can just call me Kathryn. Especially in private," Kathryn told me with a warm smile. "This is the closest I get to a vacation, so I won't have you ruining it by making me feel like I'm working."

"Okay, Ms... Kathryn." It felt strange to call her that, but I liked it. It felt like we were friends. "I'll make sure you're out of bed by noon tomorrow for the meeting."

Kathryn grinned. She had the enthusiasm of a college freshman going to her first frat party wrapped around her like clothing. I had a feeling it might be harder than I was expecting to get her up in time. "I knew it was a good idea to bring you."

Kathryn giggled and hurried out the door. I went back to my own room and looked out the window again. The ocean was calling me. I was going swimming.

THE WATER WAS EVEN BETTER than the pictures made it out to be. It was calm and clear, like looking into an aquarium. I stepped timidly out into the water and was presently surprised to find it warm. It was like bathwater. The water wasn't cold like Lake Michigan or sandy like the beach in Florida. It was exactly what I imagined a beach looked like in heaven.

I waded out to my hips before I stopped. I was slightly hesitant to get my brand new swimsuit wet. It was a deep burgundy halter top that fit like a glove with a bottom that looked like a very short skirt. I had been hesitant about wearing a bikini until Raoul put me in this one. The suit hid every flaw while still making it look like I was wearing something sexy. I never would have paid the three-hundred dollars for it myself, but it certainly seemed worth the price now that I was wearing it.

A fish darted past my leg and I giggled. I spun to watch it flit toward the shore, looking up to see a man standing on the beach watching me. He was tall with broad shoulders, wearing dark blue swim trunks and a megawatt smile. My breath caught. It couldn't possibly be, but it was. It was Aiden the Assistant. He waved and my heart went into overdrive.

With my back to the ocean, I didn't see the wave coming. It shoved me forward and knocked my knees out from under me. I felt like an idiot, knowing that Aiden was there, watching me fumble through the water like a drowned cat. That was not the impression I had been going for.

"You okay, Lena?"

He was suddenly there, holding my elbow and helping stand. I wasn't sure if I was happy or mortified. I loved the way his hand held onto me, and the fact that he remembered my name made me stumble again without the need of a wave.

"You remembered my name," I said, determined to keep my feet underneath me this time.

"How could I forget it, Lena the Lawyer." He hadn't let go of my arm yet and I hoped that he never did.

"Thank you, Aiden," I whispered. I wasn't sure if I meant for helping me out of the ocean or for sending me dinner. Or both.

"Apparently, I'm memorable too," he responded, grinning at his name.

"Very," I told him. I knew I was blushing as deep a red as my swimsuit. "Actually, I never got a chance to thank you for dinner. I really appreciated it."

He guided me out of the water and up onto the beach. As soon as the water no longer threatened to knock either of us over, he let me go. He turned looked me up and down with his eyes, inspecting me for damage. Having his gaze on me made my heart pound and I suddenly felt light headed.

"It was my pleasure. You sure you're all right?" he asked, taking in my wobbly, now light-headed wobbly stance.

"I'm better than fine," I assured him. I could have been bleeding from every orifice and not have cared. Being around him was intoxicating and wonderful. "You keep rescuing me."

"I didn't know carrying books counted as a rescue," he replied. I blushed harder.

"It did that day." I looked into his hazel eyes and found them just as mesmerizing as I did the first time. They had actually gotten even better. "I can't believe you're here. Are you with one of the law firms?"

Confusion crossed his handsome face for a second, but he quickly replaced it with an easy smile. "I'm with Travel, Inc."

"Oh, that makes sense." I hoped I didn't sound as ditzy as I felt. He had the ability to completely take logical thought straight out of my brain just by standing there. The fact that his shirtless chest was soaking up the sun right in front of me certainly wasn't helping my brainpower any either. I just wanted to stare at his body and drool. "It was really nice of them to have the meeting here."

He nodded, and started making his way up the beach. I followed like a happy puppy. "This way the vacation counts as a business expense. Everyone but the accountants are happy."

I laughed far too hard at his lame joke. "So what do you do at Travel, Inc. then?"

He stumbled on some sand, but recovered quickly. I smiled nervously. I didn't want him to get nervous and run off. Not after I had been thinking of him for so long.

"Not much, really," he said smoothly, as if he had never been caught off guard. "I just help out my brother."

"You mean Ben?" I asked innocently, remembering the man from before.

"What about Ben?" He glanced away from the beach and up toward the resort buildings as if he expected Ben to jump out at him.

At that moment, I stepped directly on something sharp and let out a shriek of pain. All questions about Ben were forgotten as I hopped up and down, cradling my foot and balancing on the other.

"Are you okay?" Aiden asked, anxiously, holding his arms out to steady me. I gave sincere thought to falling just so that he'd have to catch me, but decided against it. I didn't want to be a complete ditz.

"Yeah," I answered. The pain was fading, but it still hurt. "I just stepped on something sharp."

Aiden dropped to his knees a took my foot in his hand. His gentle fingers probed my flesh and I had to put my hand on his shoulder for balance because he was making my world spin with want.

"You're barefoot again," he chastised gently. "It doesn't look like you broke the skin, though. You have something against shoes?"

"You're just as barefoot as I am," I informed him. "Besides, who goes swimming with shoes?"

He chuckled and set my foot back on the sand. "You sure you're okay?"

I nodded. "It doesn't even hurt any more. You must be magic."

He rose in a smooth motion to his full height, looking down at me with those amazing eyes. I still had my hand on his shoulder and I caught the scent of his soap again. All I could think about was kissing him. His lips were so close and perfect, and there wasn't an elevator to interrupt us this time. I closed my eyes, ready to have my fantasy become a reality.

"Aiden?" A deep voice called. At his name, he turned and once again the spell was broken. My hand dropped to my side. I was beginning to think I was cursed when it came to kissing him. Ben, wearing khakis and a polo shirt and looking very professional was looking down at us from the path back to the resort. "I heard a shriek. Everything okay down there?"

"Everything's fine," Aiden assured him. I smiled at Ben, but I really just wanted to hit him. This was the second time he had interrupted a kiss.

"It's three-o'clock. We're supposed to be in a meeting," Ben reminded him.

"Dammit!" Aiden put his hand to his head and clenched his jaw, before turning to face me. "I have to go. It was really nice to see you again."

"Likewise," I replied lamely. I wasn't sure what else to say. Everything felt cliché at this point. I wanted to ask him what his plans were for later, but I knew I was too chicken to actually do it.

He turned and took two steps before pausing. I could almost hear the internal debate in his head as he stopped and then turned back around. "Would you be interested in having dinner with me tonight?"

I grinned and my heart threatened to thump out of my chest. "Only if you come with the food this time."

A blinding smile filled his features. "Excellent. I'll come pick you up at seven." He turned and hurried up the path toward his waiting boss.

"I'm in room 2172B," I called out. He looked back and flashed me that knee-melting grin again. I watched him walk away, totally checking out his ass in his swim shorts. I was going to have to call Darcie. Mashed potato guy was back!

## CHAPTER 10

"*W*ear the silver dangling earrings. They look better with the dress," Darcie told me. I held them up to the computer screen and she nodded. Ever the saint, she helped me get ready from thousands of miles away via my laptop's web-cam. It perched up on the dresser so she could see the full ensemble.

I wore a pale blue sundress with a lace overlay. I had loved it from the moment I saw it in Raoul's selection of dresses. It was flirty, sexy, and elegant all at the same time: all the things I wanted to be for tonight. I put the earrings in and stood back so Darcie could see.

"Stunning," she informed me with a smile. "You have some cute shoes, right?"

"Of course I have cute shoes," I exclaimed, putting my hands on my hips. She raised her eyebrows and popped a potato chip into her mouth. She knew me well enough to know that shoes were not my thing. "They're silver and strappy and it doesn't matter that Kathryn bought them. I still have them, okay?"

A knock on the door took my thoughts off shoes.

"He's here!" I whispered to the computer. My stomach was suddenly doing the meringue, mambo, and cha-cha-cha. Aiden was here.

"Then you should probably go answer the door," Darcie advised me with a straight face. "Have fun! Do whatever you think I would if I were single!"

I stuck out my tongue at her and closed the laptop screen. There was a second knock, and I scrambled to get to the door, nearly tripping on my shoes laying on the floor in the process. I threw it open and did my best to look nonchalant instead of nervous and flushed.

"Hi." I opened the door wider and motioned him in. He looked good enough to eat. He was wearing dark gray pants with a crisp button-up shirt, much like the outfit he had worn the day we met. I wasn't sure if he had done it on purpose, or if that just happened to be the nicest clothes he owned. Either way, he looked great.

"Hi, yourself." He smiled as he took in the dress. "You look spectacular."

"Thanks." I was giddy from the compliment. "You look spectacular, too," I said, cringing at my words after they came out. I sounded like a love-struck tween. Go me. "I just need to grab my shoes and I'll be ready."

He waited patiently as I slipped on the pair of silver pumps. The heel was higher than I was used to, with strappy ribbons that wrapped around my ankles, but they were beautiful and I felt like a princess wearing them. I couldn't walk very fast, but I didn't care. It was beautiful out and walking slow meant I got to spend more time with Aiden.

"How do you like the island?" he asked, offering me his arm to keep me steady as we walked out the door. I happily took it, even though I felt fairly steady on my feet. No way I was turning down an opportunity to touch him.

"It's amazing. I can't believe how clear the water is here," I told him. "It's completely different than anything I've ever seen before. Emma was right about this place."

"Emma?" he asked, raising his eyebrows.

"My cousin. She, um... vacationed here about a year ago." To say she "vacationed" here was putting it mildly. My cousin, Emma LaRue, had won a trip to this resort and met billionaire Jack Saunders. Their relationship had been in all the papers and tabloids for months. I didn't want to name drop my billionaire relatives, though. It felt too much like bragging. "She met her husband here and never shuts up about how awesome this place is."

"It is definitely one of my favorite places," Aiden agreed. "I know a story like that about this place, too."

"I never believed her when she described it. I didn't know it was possible for a place this beautiful to even exist." I looked around in awe. "I can see how this place helped her fall in love."

"It would be easy to fall in love here." Aiden smiled at me and I blushed a deep, deep red. It would be all to easy to fall in love in a place like this, especially with him.

"What about you? Are you enjoying the island?" I asked, changing the subject before I accidentally professed my love for him.

"I am now that you're here," he answered with a charming grin that only sped up my already frantic heart-beat. "I thought I was going to be bored this week. I don't really need to be here for this, but it makes the company look good."

I nodded. I was here for basically the same reason. I was

here to make my boss look good. It was something we had in common.

"So I'm just a distraction from boredom for you?" I teased. I felt brave around him. Like I could say and do anything. I wasn't afraid to flirt with him, which was a new feeling for me.

"Yes. I mean, no. I mean..." He glared at me. "You certainly are distracting."

I giggled as we entered the restaurant. It was strangely quiet, and I noticed that nearly every table was empty. The clock on the wall said that it was dinner time, and I knew this was the main restaurant, but I had no idea where all the people where.

"Where is everyone?" I asked, peeking around a corner. Only one or two tables had guests at them.

"Probably hiding from me," he joked. I didn't quite get it, but he had already pulled out the schedule of events from his pocket. "Ah ha. There's a 'Welcome to the Island' party going on at the dance club." He put the schedule back neatly into his jacket. "Would you like to go there instead?"

"And have to deal with drunk lawyers and loud music?" I quickly shook my head. "This looks like more fun."

He looked around at the quiet, candlelit tables and nodded. "I think so, too."

The host showed us to a small, romantic table for two next to the window. The sun was just setting on the horizon and turning everything into red and orange flame. We had the best seat in the house since no one else was in the restaurant. It was absolutely stunning. I couldn't imagine a better place to spend an evening with an attractive man.

"What are you getting?" I asked after we had both taken a moment to look through the heavy leather menus. There was some amazing, fancy sounding food and I wanted to try all of it.

"I have no idea," he answered honestly, peering at the menu. "It all looks good. What about you?"

"I'm in the same boat. I think I'll just have one of everything." I looked up at him from the menu. "It's all inclusive, right?"

He chuckled and set his menu down, focusing his beautiful eyes on me. I felt like I was the center of the entire universe when he looked at me. "Why don't we order for each other?"

"What do you mean?" I asked, setting my menu down as well.

"It's something my brother and I used to do as kids," he explained. "I'd pick his meal and he'd pick mine."

I thought about what I would order for my sister and wondered just what kind of terrible things he had eaten doing this. "What's to stop you from picking something terrible? I know my sister would have picked the most disgusting thing on the menu for me just because it would be funny."

"Nothing," he said with a shrug. "I've eaten some disgusting things because of my brother. But, if we ordered it, my Dad made us eat it. Neither of us could leave until our meals were finished. So, in order to avoid the wrath of Dad, we usually ordered good things for each other. It was easier than the alternative."

"Your dad sounds strict," I said. I couldn't imagine my dad doing something like that. He would have let my sister and I reorder until we got something we liked. There was a reason my dad called us his princesses.

"My Dad's not a bad guy," Aiden replied quickly.

"There's a reason he's as successful as he is. He's just... demanding."

"What does your dad do?" I asked. I imagined that his successful father was what had gotten him such a cushy assistant position.

"He's a businessman. He wants me to follow in his foot-steps, but I don't want the same things he does." He shrugged. "The danger of having successful parents is that they expect successful children."

I bit my lip as an awkward silence came between us. I knew the burden of a parent's wishes. Despite the fact that I had more education and training than either of my parents, they let their disappointment show that I was just a para-legal one too many times for me to forget. Family was a hard topic for a date.

"Prime rib with mashed potatoes. Veggies on the side," I blurted out. Aiden's brows came together over hazel eyes. I smiled nervously and explained, "that's what I'm picking for you."

A slow, warm smile filled his face and fanned my current level of infatuation for him up another level. "Okay..." He held up his menu, peeking over the top of it every couple seconds as if he were trying to read what I would want off my face. Finally, he put the menu down. "Lobster ravioli with champagne butter sauce."

"I was kind of hoping you would pick that," I admitted with a grin. "I love the idea of a champagne butter sauce. I have no idea what it is, but is sounds delicious."

"I'm excited for the prime rib. It's one of my favorites." He smiled, making my world go bright again. "Why'd you pick it?"

I opened my mouth, ready to tell him that it just sounded manly, but I decided I should tell him the real reason, even if it gave away more than I wanted. "My grandmother."

"You managed to call her and ask without me noticing?" he teased.

"No," I said knowing a blush was creeping across my cheeks. "My grandmother was the epitome of the conventional 1950's housewife and she firmly believed that the way to a man's heart was through his stomach. She decided that the reason I wasn't married was that I didn't know how to cook properly. So she tried to teach me how to cook her husband-winning prime rib."

He leaned back in his chair, obviously enjoying my story, so I continued.

"She spent an entire day teaching me all her cooking secrets." I smiled fondly at the memory. I could still see her smiling in that kitchen when I closed my eyes. "I failed miserably at cooking the prime rib, but we had the most amazing day together- just talking and laughing. I learned just how much she loved me and that she was proud of me. Really proud of me- even though I wasn't married. She just wanted me to be happy."

"She sounds wonderful." He cocked his head slightly to the side, a small smile on his face as he watched me remember.

"She was. She died a week later." I forced a smile to banish the heartache I always felt at her passing. "Anyway, I ordered the prime rib because she would have liked you. She would have wanted me to make it for you, but you really don't want to eat mine."

"So, you're using your grandmother's secret of prime rib to catch me?" he asked slowly, letting the implication of my story come out in the open.

I blushed even harder and opened my mouth to protest,

but his knowing smile told me it was futile. "Maybe a little bit," I conceded.

"Then I hope the prime rib here is as good as your grandmother's," he said. A little tremor of hope and excitement went through me. He wanted me to catch him.

"Good evening, folks," a little blonde waitress announced, coming up to the table and pouring us waters. "I'll be your server this evening. What can I get you?"

"My beautiful date here will have the lobster ravioli with champagne butter sauce," he informed her. A thrill went down my spine at the compliment.

"Excellent choice, sir. And for you?"

Aiden looked at me, waiting for me to order. "He'll have the prime rib with mashed potatoes," I said quickly.

"Another excellent choice, ma'am" the waitress replied, jotting it down on a little notepad. "Anything to drink? Some wine perhaps?"

I looked at him and shrugged. I hadn't even looked at the wine menu.

"The Trentino Pinot Grigio for her, and the d'Arenberg Shira for me please," he requested. I liked that he sounded extremely confident in selecting something, especially since I hadn't seen him even look at the wine menu. "Bring the bottles, please."

"Excellent again. I'll be back in just a moment with your wine, sir" she said before hurrying off to put in our orders. The staff was so formal and polite with all the sirs and ma'ams. I certainly felt rich.

"Trentino Pinot Grigio?" I asked, picking up the wine menu from the table. I had no idea what that was.

"It's an Italian, dry white wine with light undertones. It will match your lobster nicely," he explained. "I could get champagne if you prefer, but I didn't want it to compete with the sauce."

I set down the wine menu without even looking all the way through it for my wine. "No, that sounds great. You know a lot about wine?"

"It's a hobby." He shrugged the nonchalant shrug of someone who is actually an expert. "I eat out a lot-- lots of business meetings-- so I started paying attention and talking with the sommelier."

I nodded. I only knew that a sommelier was the wine expert at fancy restaurants because Emma had talked about them. I had a feeling that working with Kathryn, I would begin to meet them at her business dinners. One of the perks of working for wealthy bosses was getting to have nice things.

The waitress returned then with two bottles of wine and accompanying ice buckets. She quickly uncorked his first, and handed him the cork when he stretched out his hand. He smelled it while she poured a small amount of red wine into his glass, then waited.

He spun the liquid in the glass slowly, his eyes taking in every detail of the rich red liquid. He inhaled the vapors like a perfume and then tasted it, rolling the wine around on his tongue. "Perfect," he said, finally.

She smiled and added more wine to his glass before placing the bottle in an ice bucket next to our table. She then repeated the motions with my white wine. I did my best to mimic Aiden's steps.

"It's good," I said. It smelled good, but tasted like regular white wine. I wasn't sure what I was supposed to be looking for. The waitress finished pouring my glass and set the bottle into the second ice bucket.

"Your food will be out shortly," she informed us, and then hurried off.

"What do you think?" Aiden asked as I took another sip of wine.

I fiddled with the stem of my wine glass before answering. "Honestly? I don't know anything about wine and I have no idea what I just did."

He took a sip of his red. "Would you like to?"

I nodded and he smiled. He turned and snagged two empty wine glasses from the table behind him and set them on the table. "We'll start with yours. First, look at the bottle. Evaluate the shape, the size and it's condition. Then look at the cork. The cork tells you a lot about the wine. Is it a nice cork? Is it cheaply made? Does it smell good?"

I pulled the cork from the wine bottle and inhaled the scent. "It smells good. And it's not falling apart, so I guess that means it's a good cork?"

"Yes," he said with a nod. "Though, the cork is becoming less important as wineries shift to plastic or even screw-top to prevent corked wine."

"Corked wine?" I asked.

"Where the cork has contaminated the wine," he explained.

"Oh, okay." I held up the cork. "This does not have that."

"Next, the sample." Aiden poured a small amount of the golden liquid into an empty wine glass. "Look at the wine. Look at the color. It tells you about maturity and quality. Color changes with age--whites darken and reds lighten. It should also be clear and not have anything floating in it."

The wine looked golden and soft. I couldn't see anything wrong so I nodded for him to continue.

"Now, swirl." He demonstrated the gentle rocking motion with his wrist. "See how it runs down the glass?

Those are the 'legs'. The faster they run down the side, the less alcohol and body it will have. Long legs indicate a fuller body and more alcohol."

"How do my legs compare?" I asked, looking at my wine and trying to decide if the liquid was moving fast or slow. I didn't even think of the sexual implication until he bent to the side and lifted up the table cloth.

"You have short legs, though very nice ones. Much like your wine." Aiden winked and flashed me a cocky smile that made my stomach flutter.

I blushed, embarrassed that I had walked so blindly into that, but took the compliment.

"Now, the most important part: the smell." Aiden watched as I put the open glass to my nose and inhaled. "Swirling it helps aerate the wine and increase the smell. Close your eyes and tell me what you smell."

"I smell... wine." I opened my eyes, feeling defeated.

"Try again," he coached.

I took one last look at him and closed my eyes. I needed to concentrate. "I smell... apples. Green apples." I opened my eyes, surprised at the new scent in my wine.

He grinned. "Good. What else?"

"Citrus. It reminds me of limes," I said hesitantly. I didn't want to be wrong.

"Perfect. Now taste it," he instructed. " Just a small taste, let it run across your tongue and fill your senses."

I tried not to squirm as I thought of the erotic implications of that sentence. I would like to run him across my tongue and have him fill my senses. I kept my eyes closed, knowing that he would see all my lusty thoughts if I opened them. "It's not sweet, but crisp. I can taste the apple in it. There's no burn at the end like some wines have."

"Excellent," he praised me. I opened my eyes to see him

staring at me. There was a small pride and a lot of desire in that gaze. A deep need in my core started ache for him.

"Can I try yours?" I asked, setting my glass down.

"Please," he responded, obviously glad I wanted to try more. "Have a sip of water and then try it." I sipped on my water to clear the taste of the first wine before he handed me the bottle and a new glass.

My hands shook a little as I poured a small amount and narrated my actions. "The bottle is pretty. The cork looks and smells good." I set the bottle and cork down and picked up the wine glass to swirl. "Yours has longer legs than mine, which is true it both cases."

Aiden chuckled and I grinned at him before closing my eyes to smell the wine.

"I smell... pepper. And soil." I opened my eyes and looked at him. "But it's a good soil smell, not like *dirt* dirt. It smells drinkable."

Aiden laughed. "Good. Try it and see what you think."

I took a small sip, hoping his eyes were on my lips. The idea that he was watching my mouth made my female parts ache for his touch. "It's got a dark, fruity taste." I scrunched my nose. "And it's got that bitter wine taste at the end."

"Those are tanins. You'll learn to love them," he promised. "Do you like it?"

"It's good." I took another small sip, liking the first part but not the tanins.

"Do you want more?" he asked, watching my face but keeping his laughter to himself.

"No, thank you," I answered. "I like mine better."

Just then our food arrived. The waitress set it down in front of us, made sure we were happy and then disappeared to leave us alone once again. I took a bite and instantly found my way to food heaven.

"This is delicious," I moaned. "How's yours?"

He cut off a small piece, put it on his fork, and then held it out for me to eat. I only hesitated for a second before leaning forward and taking it in my mouth.

"It's perfect. Grandma would be proud," I told him, enjoy the tender piece of meat.

"I agree," he said with a grin. He took another bite.

"Why'd you pick the lobster for me?" I asked, taking a sip of wine before going back to my dinner.

He paused for a moment, then shrugged. "I just thought it would impress you. Lobster in a champagne butter sauce sounds fancy and awesome. I don't have a good story for it."

"What? No story?" I teased.

"I did tell you the origin of the game," he countered. "That has to count for something."

I laughed, enjoying his honesty. "Well, it's delicious. Want some?" I held out a my fork with a bite prepared for him. He took it carefully in his teeth. I liked that the next bite I took would have him on it.

"I think your grandma would approve of that as well," he said quietly. I grinned. I knew she would most certainly approve, and it had nothing to do with the food.

## CHAPTER 11

*A*iden took my hand in his as we left the restaurant. The night air was still tropically warm and the ocean breeze ruffled my skirt. This truly was paradise.

"Walk on the beach with me?" Aiden asked, pulling me gently toward the sound of water. I would have followed him willingly into a volcano. A moonlit walk on the beach was better than I could have dreamed.

"That sounds great," I agreed. It only took us a moment to reach the sand. My heels immediately sank and I knew I would twist an ankle if I stayed on them. "Hold on, I need to take my shoes off to walk in the sand."

"Barefoot again?" he teased gently as he also removed his shoes. He finished nearly as soon as I did, standing beside me in the sand. "How tall are those heels?"

"Tall?" I shrugged. I had no idea the actual height, just that they were taller than my usual selection of heels.

"I like you this height better," he told me. A warm flush went through me. No one had ever said that to me before. I always thought I was too short and needed heels.

"Really? I thought guys liked the tall, leggy blondes best."

"I can't do this with a tall, leggy blonde," he informed me, stepping close and draping his arm over my shoulder. Goosebumps and want skittered across my skin. I could barely believe that this handsome, funny, man was holding me on a moonlit beach. It seemed too good to be true.

The sand was soft and warm under my feet. The travel guides hadn't been kidding when they raved about Caribbean sand. The moon was rising slowly and casting pale, silver light on every wave. Everything had a magical glow that made anything seem possible.

"You said you have a brother," I said as we walked. I wanted to know everything about Aiden. "Any other siblings?"

"Just Logan," he replied. "You?"

"A younger sister." I smiled thinking of her. "Are you and your brother close?"

"We work together, so kind of. We were really close when we were little, but when I left for college we grew apart." He pulled me closer to him, as if he were searching for my warmth in the dark.

"You said your brother's name is Logan?"

"Yeah." He paused and looked at me. "Why?"

"You're going to laugh, but I thought Ben was your brother."

"Because we look so much alike, right?" Aiden puffed out his chest and tried to make himself bigger. All he managed to do was make himself look ridiculous.

"Yeah, I should have thought of that," I agreed, giggling as he ape walked down the beach. Ben was just an over-bearing boss, not a concerned brother. "You just said you worked with your brother, and I assumed."

"I do work with my brother. He works for Travel, Inc. as well." He grinned at me. "You might even call it a family business."

"I would love to work at the same company as my sister," I said honestly.

"Working with family isn't all it's cracked up to be." The easy laughter was gone, replaced by a bitter humor. "It makes it hard to fire anyone, even if they do a terrible job."

"What about your mom?" I asked quietly, curiosity getting the better of me.

"She died when I was twelve. Dad wasn't exactly good with kids." He shrugged as if it didn't bother him, but the slight tension in his voice belied the truth.

"I'm sorry." I wasn't sure what else to say. I wanted to hold him close and take away all the pain that was edging into his voice.

"It was a long time ago," he assured me, his eyes still distant.

"I'm still sorry," I said quietly. I wrapped my arm around his waist and pulled him closer to me. His arm tightened, and didn't let go. I wished I could carry some of the pain that obviously weighed heavy on his shoulders. I tried to think of something I could say or do to make him smile again.

We walked in silence for a moment until I tripped on yet another rock. Aiden caught me easily, preventing me from falling to the sand. Wrapped in his arms and dizzy with want from having him this close, my heart beat raced out of control. He was so damn handsome. The moonlight high-lighted his strong jawline and striking features, while his eyes seemed to capture the pale light of the moon and reflect only beauty.

"You and those rocks just don't seem to get along," he murmured quietly, smiling down at me in his arms.

"It's a good thing you're here to rescue me then," I whispered, staring at his mouth. It was sensuous and made for kissing. Every fiber of my being wanted to taste him. I half expected Ben to pop out of nowhere and ruin the moment for a third time.

Aiden tipped his head and slowly lowered his lips to mine. My world spun in a kaleidoscope of color as we finally connected. His lips were soft and receptive. He tasted like sunshine and wine. I honestly couldn't get enough of him, and used my tongue to draw him in further. I wanted to stay wrapped up in moonlight and his arms, tasting his mouth on mine and loving every second of it.

"Wow," I whispered when we finally had to break apart or suffocate.

"Wow, indeed," he agreed, his voice rough and shaky. His eyes sparkled with delight. Apparently he had enjoyed kissing me as much as I did him.

"Would you like a drink at my place? It's just over there," I offered. I wasn't really interested in a drink, but it was the perfect excuse to get him to stay with me. Maybe even kiss me again. Heat surged through my veins at the thought of him kissing me again.

He didn't even look up at the direction I indicated. "I'd love one," he said, his voice husky and eyes hungry.

He released me enough to let me lead the way to the glass doors of my hotel suite. I dropped my shoes on the porch and slid the keycard in. I was really, really glad that I didn't leave my laundry out on the bed. I usually left my clothing scattered across the bed when I traveled, but I didn't want to clutter the beautiful room this time. I patted past-me on the head. She had done a good thing.

"Leave it open," Aiden commanded once we were inside. I dropped my hand from the door as I looked out at the moonlit waves. A cool breeze ruffled the filmy curtains, filling the room with the scent of water and night flowers. I nodded and was suddenly back in Aiden's arms.

His hands went to my hips, bringing him to me like a dance partner. I stopped to take in his strong cheekbones, his wind-ruffled hair, and the column of his throat leading down to a perfectly sculpted chest. I almost couldn't believe this was happening. This was too good to be true.

I cautiously unbuttoned the top button of his shirt, watching his face. If this was all in my head, this was the point I would wake up. My dreams never let me get past this point and get to the good stuff. If I was going to wake up from this dream, it was now.

The button slid free and the corner of Aiden's mouth rose in a cocky, sexy-as-hell smirk. He knew how much I wanted him. He knew it and was enjoying it. I undid the next button down and his hands tightened on my waist. He pulled my hips to his, his eyes darkening with want as our bodies touched. I could now feel the proof of just how much want pressing into my stomach. It made my knees go to jelly.

He leaned forward and kissed the corner of my mouth, then glided his tongue to the center of my lips. I trembled, opening my mouth to give him access and quickly finishing the buttons. He shrugged out of his shirt and let it fall to the floor. His tank-top undershirt was in the way of me touching his skin, so I pulled it up over his head. My hands caressed perfect abs and sculpted pecs in the process. I moaned without realizing it.

He was all heat and muscle. Strong lines of sinew and strength under smooth skin that were built for my fingers to trace. I could feel his heart pounding under my fingertips, as I touched his chest. It was steady and strong, but obviously as excited as I was.

He kissed me again, drawing my tongue to his. I skimmed my hands up his perfect body, up to his neck and into that delicious hair. My fingers fisted into his gentle curls, holding him in my kiss. The way his body responded to mine was intoxicating.

His hands moved from my hips to my ass where he started to hike up my skirt. I felt his smile through our kiss as his fingers touched bare skin. The touch made my hips rock into his, my body questing for more. He groaned softly, telling me without words just how much he wanted this.

His hands still on my ass, he shuffled his feet forward. I followed his lead until the back of my knees touched the bed. I arched my hips against him and he shuddered with want. With a gentle push from him, I let go of his hair, and tumbled onto the mattress.

He looked down at me, his gaze full of pure desire. His mouth opened slightly and then curved up in that cocky grin that made my panties moisten. I arched my hips up to tempt him and the smile grew more confident. Slowly, he went to his knees on the floor by the bed.

My knees bent over the edge of the mattress and Aiden used his broad shoulders to separate them. He made sure I was watching, those hazel eyes burning just above my skirt, before beginning my pleasure. He kissed up from my bare feet, up my calf, up my thigh and increasing my temperature with every kiss.

His fingers hooked around the tiny string of my panties' waistband and he pulled them off with a smooth, practiced motion.

"Pretty," he said, holding them up in the air to admire them before tossing them to the side. "But they have to go."

I was breathless with anticipation as he used just one finger to trace the curve of my upper thigh. I couldn't see anything with my dress still in the way, so I had no idea what he was going to do next. I reached down and pulled the skirt back, wanting to see everything, but he shook his head and put it right back up.

Nervousness and excitement battled in my chest. I wanted to go wherever he led. I closed my eyes and did my best to relax, but knowing he was going to do wonderful things to me made it hard not to squirm with anticipation.

He kissed one inner thigh, and then the other. His cheeks were smooth and I knew he must have shaved just for dinner. Something about the idea of him shaving just for me felt special.

His lips kissed the V at the top of my legs and I jerked at the surge of pleasure. I was so wound with lust that even the barest breath against my pleasure center would have sent shivers down my spine. A full kiss was like being struck my lightning.

He chuckled, nuzzling my inner thigh and tightening his grip on my hips. He did it again and I moaned into the night. His lips applied pressure while his teeth and tongue worked magic. I had never had anything this wonderful in my life. He coaxed me gently to the edge of what I could take.

"Aiden," I whimpered as I started to shake. At his name, he slid one finger inside of me, sliding in on my excitement. With a flick of his tongue and finger in unison, he turned my whimper into a full moan, shooting me into pure bliss.

White energy scorched the edges of my vision and Aiden showed me heaven. I crashed back to earth, gasping and spinning. When I opened my eyes, he was watching me. Lust burned in his eyes with a fire I wanted inside of me.

I sat up and released the zipper to wiggle out of my dress. His pupils dilated as he watched the lacy dress clear my head. I loved the way he looked at my body like I was the sexiest thing he had ever seen. He wanted me in a way that made me writhe with want.

Slowly, he stood and pulled a square package from his pocket while I undid his belt and pants. With a strong tug, I released him from his clothing. He kicked his pants and briefs to the side, giving me a look at what I was getting. His body, long and hard in the moonlight, made me shiver with desire.

He put one knee up on the bed beside me as he reached behind me to undo the bra clasp on my back. I giggled when he didn't find it.

"It's on the front," I whispered, looking up at him.

His eyebrows raised and he grinned. "That's even better."

He moved his hand from my back to my shoulder, pushing me to lay down on the bed. I couldn't decide if I wanted to close my eyes and savor the moment, or keep them open and watch. I looked up at Aiden and knew I wanted to watch.

He undid the snap between my breasts and his breathing grew faster as he pulled the bra apart. His right hand cupped my exposed breast and he ran his thumb across the nipple. It pebbled under his touch and sent a bolt of want and desire straight from his fingertip down to my now throbbing center of need.

"Please?" I begged, writhing under his touch and needing so much more. "Please don't make me wait..."

He reached for the foil package and I waited in breathless agony until he was poised at my entrance.

"Lena," he whispered. Our eyes locked and he entered.

It was like a puzzle piece finally clicking into place. He was made for me and I for him. My body moved to greet his without having to think. Together we arched and writhed as he explored my depths.

The muscles of his back tightened as as he worked, keeping a stead pace that drove me wild. I moaned, feeling like I could float away on pleasure just by what he was doing to me. It was as if he had always known every secret of my body and was using them to push me to the limits of what I could tolerate and beyond. It was ecstasy.

My legs started to shake as he took me higher. I dug my fingernails into his back, pulling those muscles further into me. I needed all of him.

"Come for me," he whispered, the desire raw in his voice. It was all I needed to push me flying over the edge yet again.

Pulsing pleasure flooded my nerves, but he didn't stop. Tucking one leg up under his shoulder, he increased his rhythm. As I came back to the moment, I reveled in the effect I was having on him. His breathing was fast and ragged, and his brow was concentrated with lust. I could feel the need coursing through his hand on my breast and thigh.

Our eyes found each other in the night.

"Aiden..."

"Lena..."

I could tell he was trying his best to hold back, to make this last. I wanted him more than I wanted to breathe. I wanted him to explode like I did and to lose himself in me.

"Come for me," I repeated back his own phrase.

Primal need flashed through his beautiful eyes as he

thrust and shuddered. I arched my hips to take him, pulling him deeper into me. I never wanted to let him go. I wanted him to remain with me like this forever.

After a perfect moment of eternity, he collapsed forward. He felt heavy and strong on top of me, and I loved it. He was an Aiden blanket of perfection.

"You're amazing," he gasped. We were both covered in sweat and breathing hard. I certainly felt amazing. He slowly raised himself up to look at me. Hazel eyes roved my body, taking in every detail and wanting more. "And so beautiful."

I grinned up at him. "You're not too bad yourself."

"Not too bad?" He raised an eyebrow at my bold statement. "I'm pretty sure I just rocked your world."

It would have sounded cocky if it hadn't been true. To be honest, my world was still rocking. I kissed him, loving the way he tasted and the feel of his skin against mine.

"Care to rock it again?" I asked.

He grinned and proceeded to rock my universe.

## CHAPTER 12

*W*arm yellow sunshine and a soft breeze off the ocean woke me. I kept my eyes closed for a moment, afraid that the night before had been nothing but a wonderful dream. When I did finally open my eyes, I was relieved to see it wasn't. Aiden lay in bed next to me, his soft hazel gaze as warm as the sunshine. He had his phone out and was typing on the slide-out keyboard, but he was definitely paying more attention to me than his phone.

"Were you watching me sleep?" I asked, drowsily.

"Maybe." He smiled and set his phone to the side. "You just look so peaceful and happy."

"Probably because I am." I stretched my arms up over my head, keenly aware of his eyes taking in the seductive motion. "What time is it?"

"A little past eleven," he said, checking his watch. "You want some breakfast?"

Panic woke me from my happy, lazy morning slumber. "I can't! I have a meeting and Kathryn asked me to make sure she's prepped!"

I stumbled out of bed, pulling the bed sheet with me

and wrapping it around my nakedness. I knew he had seen me naked, but that had been in the forgiving moonlight and with wine. I wasn't sure I was ready for the harsh details of daylight.

Aiden let me take the sheet, chuckling as I wrapped it around me like some sort of oversized toga. He stayed on the bed, stretched out and gloriously naked. He looked even better in the sunshine. Moonlight was good, but sunlight revealed so many more wonderful things about his body. There were freckles across his shoulders and a trail of golden hair from his belly button south to heaven. If I had been wearing panties, seeing him naked in my bed would have melted them.

I ran to the drawer where I had put my underthings. I had to get out of the room before he could seduce me with the delicious V his hipbones sat at the top of. He put his arms behind his head, chuckling when I nearly tripped on the sheet. With his arms up above his head, his biceps flexed and his broad shoulders stood defined against the dark wood of the headboard. I forgot what I was doing.

His mouth twitched upwards and he displayed himself even more as I stared. I dropped the sheet and chucked it at him. "You're distracting me," I informed him as I slipped into a bra and matching panties.

"I can do more than just distract," he teased. His mouth curled into a naughty, seductive grin that matched the desire in his eyes.

"That's tempting...very tempting," I moaned as he showed me just how distracting he could be. I shook my head, hating that I was going to leave this perfect specimen of a man alone in my bed to go to a meeting. "I'm going to be late!'

He laughed and tried again, his masculinity rising to

tempt me. My body ached to have him fill me again like he did last night. I wanted to feel that again and again and again. My resolve weakened and a little whimper of want escaped me.

"Don't you have to go to this thing too?" I whined, wanting to drop the suit I had picked out and jump on the bed with him instead.

"Nope." His eyes were dark with lust as he looked at me. "This one is just for you lucky lawyers."

I closed my eyes and pulled up Kathryn's face. What would she do? She would go to the meeting. I could do this. She was counting on me to be there.

I put my shirt over my head and then peeked open an eye to look at him again. Who was I kidding? Any woman in her right mind would have gone back to that bed as soon as she saw him naked. I put on my pants and a pair of flats, trying not to think about what I was doing.

"You have some serious willpower," he said as I quickly brushed my hair and threw on some mascara. He sounded impressed.

"You have no idea how much I want to stay here instead." I came over to him, leaning over so I could kiss him before I left. He tangled his fingers into my hair, pulling my mouth into his and showing me with his tongue just what I would be missing out on. When he released me, I was breathless and flushed. "Will you be here when I get back?"

"Maybe. Depends on if I find another hot lawyer walking around shoeless," he teased.

I forced out a laugh as I turned to face the window. I knew he was just joking, but it felt all too possible. He was so incredibly handsome, charming, and amazing in the sack. Women must fall into his bed all the time. I had no idea what had made me one of them, and I was terrified that he would find someone else to fall with. There was nothing that made me special.

I went to the door and looked back as I put my hand on the handle. He was still splayed out on the bed in all his muscular glory. If I looked much longer I was going to spontaneously combust with want. "I'll see you later, then?"

"Count on it." He smiled from the bed, making my knees weaken. "Have fun at the meeting."

I stepped outside and leaned against the closed door, trying to put my wits back together. I was still strongly considering abandoning Kathryn and going back in there to lick those abs like they were candy. The idea made me all warm and gooey in the all the right places, but I had a job to do. Kathryn was counting on me and I refused to let her down. Besides, I wanted to keep my job and the future it promised more than I wanted an hour or two of pleasure. Though, the pleasure was certainly giving the future a good run for its money.

THE CONFERENCE ROOM was dimly lit as I set up Kathryn's laptop for the PowerPoint presentation. Several of the representatives from the other law firms were already there, but they were sitting quietly sipping at strong coffees. The party last night must have been wild. I was overdressed compared to their casual shorts and t-shirts, but that was fine by me. I looked the part of a lawyer here.

Kathryn came in five minutes before the meeting was supposed to start. I had woken her up and gotten her coffee on my way to get things set up. With her big sunglasses still on in the dark room and clutching her coffee like a lifeline, she looked miserable. The rest of the lawyers stumbled into the conference room behind her, several of them hung over or possibly still drunk.

"Have a good night?" I asked, handing Kathryn her notes.

"I haven't drank like that since law school," she admitted, shaking her head and then wincing at the motion. "Probably because I haven't drank with William since law school."

"William?" I raised my eyebrows.

"The cute one in the dark gray shorts," she whispered, pointing to a man in the front row.

"The one that looks like Robert Redford?" I asked. She grinned and I could see the sparkle in her eyes even through the dark glasses.

"Except William has aged even better." She sipped her coffee. "Do you know if the representative for Travel, Inc. is on the island yet?"

"Yes, he has," I informed her. "I actually had dinner with his assistant last night."

"His assistant?" Kathryn frowned and then shrugged it off. "I didn't know he had one."

"His name's Aiden." I couldn't keep the smile out of my voice. I looked at Kathryn to see if she recognized the name, but she was too busy making eyes with William. I wasn't even sure she had heard me say anything. I touched her shoulder to get her attention. "You ready for the presentation?"

"I could do this in my sleep," she replied, finally taking off her sunglasses. " Besides, half the people here are too hung over to remember it anyway. Remind me to schedule this meeting in the afternoon next year."

I handed her the clicker for the slide show and took a seat in the back.

"Attention, everyone," Kathryn announced. Her voice was clear and commanding. "Time to at least look like you're earning your paychecks."

I chuckled and leaned back in my chair to watch. Even hung over, Kathryn was a force to be reckoned with.

## CHAPTER 13

*I* hurried back to my room, hoping to find Aiden still stretched out naked on my bed. The meeting had been relatively quick, and now the idea of walking in and jumping on the bed with him had me practically sprinting.

I stepped into the room with a huge grin on my face, only to have it fall off. The bed was made and he was gone. I had only been away for a little while and the meeting had gotten out early. Maybe he did go find another barefoot lawyer. My shoulders slumped.

The room phone rang and I shuffled my feet to answer it. Probably just housekeeping asking if I wanted turn-down service. "Hello?"

"Lena?" Aiden's voice crackled across the line.

"Aiden?" I hoped the almost absurd amount of happiness in my voice didn't scare him off.

"You want to go fishing with me?" he asked.

"Fishing?" I repeated, making sure I had heard the correct word.

"Do I have to answer in the form of a question?" I could

hear the smile in his voice. "Yes, fishing. I have a boat at the docks and the weather is beautiful."

I thought about it for a moment. I had never really understood the appeal of putting worms on a hook and hoping something ate one, but the idea of spending the afternoon out on the water with Aiden sounded absolutely fantastic. "Sure! Let me change and I'll be right there."

"Okay," he said, sounding excited. "Dock two. I'll see you soon."

I hung up the phone and did a happy dance across the room. I had the rest of the day to play with my new favorite person. I quickly changed into a cute, red two-piece with polka dots, a pair of board shorts, and a light t-shirt. Sunscreen and a towel went in a bag and with a pair of sandals on my feet, I was out the door in no time.

I easily found the dock on the water's edge. Aiden waved to me from the bow of a speed boat and I hurried over to him. The boat was painted a sparkly, deep blue and had two leather seats in the front and a larger square area in the back where we could sit and fish.

"Ahoy, matey," Aiden called out as I came over. I grinned.

"Ahoy," I repeated, feeling like a pirate. "Permission to come aboard?"

Aiden grinned and reached a hand out over the boat. "Permission most certainly granted."

I took his hand, soaking in the warmth and strength as he helped me up onto the boat deck. My sandals slipped on the smooth surface of the deck, but he kept me up. I gave him a bashful grin.

"It's easier if you just go barefoot," he advised. I noticed he wasn't wearing shoes either, so I slipped them off and tucked them into my bag. "Ready?"

I nodded and together we sat down in the two leather

seats in the front of the boat. The engine purred to life and he carefully navigated us out into open water.

"Where'd you get the boat?" I asked, pulling my hair up into a ponytail. "It's nice."

"I rented it from the resort," he explained. The water was darker as we went out further, but still just as clear. "I know a great little fishing spot not too far from here. Ready?"

"Sure," I replied, peering down at the water. It looked like I could reach out and touch the bottom of the ocean the water was so clear, but I had a feeling that it was far deeper than I could reach. "I hope you're not spending all your money on me."

"Don't you worry about what I'm spending," he chastised. "It all gets written off by the company anyway. Just enjoy yourself and don't think too much."

Aiden revved the engine and the boat took off. I squealed in delight at the sudden speed as we zoomed across the water. The wind and spray of the ocean were exhilarating. I giggled as he zigged and zagged through the waves, turning tight circles and catching air off some of the waves. My hair streamed out behind me and my eyes watered from the speed, but I didn't want him to stop. I loved it.

All too soon he slowed the boat to the original slow putter before stopping it completely. I could just barely see the faint outline of the island on the horizon. Other than some birds and the fish, the two of us were completely alone in a world of blue sky and sapphire water. It was suddenly very quiet without the roar of the engine and the wind rushing past my ears.

"That was awesome," I said breathlessly. My face hurt from smiling so wide. "Where did you learn to do that?"

"One of the guys I went to college with had a brother

who was really into sailing. I spent a lot of time out on the water with him."

"This isn't exactly a sailboat," I said, looking at the very important lack of sail on our speedboat.

"I know," Aiden replied with a grin. "His brother and I would specifically take out a speedboat just to piss him off."

Aiden stood from the driver's seat and went to the back of the boat. I followed him with my eyes as he lifted one of the seat cushions in the back and pulled out a picnic basket. "You hungry?"

My stomach growled, answering for me. "I guess so," I replied with a laugh.

I moved carefully to the back of the boat to sit on the bench next to Aiden. He placed the basket on the floor and began to pull out food. There were sandwiches, chips, several cans of soda, cookies, and a big bowl of fresh fruit.

"I didn't know what kind of sandwich you would want," he told me as he pulled out more sandwiches than we could possibly eat. "So I got turkey, PB&J, and ham. Condiments are all on the side."

"I'm a PB&J kind of girl, but turkey is a good second," I said choosing one of the plastic wrapped sandwiches. "This looks wonderful. Thank you."

"You are very welcome. I guess that means more ham and cheese sandwiches for me," he replied with a grin. He picked a ham sandwich up and immediately squirted four packets of mustard onto the bread. I raised my eyebrows and gave the sandwich a sidewise look. It was a lot of mustard.

He shrugged. "What? I like mustard."

I laughed, and I dug into my peanut butter and jelly with gusto.

"So, I told you about my brother and father," Aiden said

after a moment of quiet. "What about your family? You said you have a sister?"

I swallowed the last bite of my sandwich and reached for the bag of chips. "My parents, Lou and Mina, were high-school sweethearts. My sister, Louisa, just started college. It's a three hour drive, so I haven't seen much of her since she left home."

"Your parents are Lou and Mina," he repeated, enunciating their names carefully. "And they have two daughters named Louisa and Lena?"

"Yup." I nodded slowly. We had gotten plenty of grief through our lives on the similarity of all our names. "They wanted to name our dog Lucina, but Louisa and I decided to name her Casey."

Aiden laughed, taking out another sandwich and again applying a ridiculous amount of mustard. "You close with your parents?"

I shrugged. "I guess. They live just outside Chicago, so I try and see them when I can. Work keeps me pretty busy, though."

He nodded. His work must keep him busy as well. He pulled out another sandwich, drenching it with mustard before digging in.

"What about you? What does your dad think of you working for Travel, Inc.?" I asked, taking a handful of chips.

He chewed slowly before finally swallowing. "It's complicated." His tone of voice told me that it wasn't really something he wanted to discuss.

"Oh." I chewed on my lip for a moment, trying to think of something that he would want to talk about. His dad was definitely a sore subject with him. "What's your favorite place that you've gone to for work? Besides here, I mean."

"This is definitely one of my favorite places," Aiden

replied, his shoulders relaxing and the easy smile coming back to the corners of his eyes.

"Las Vegas? Tokyo?" I watched as he shook his head. Where would a man as handsome and charming as Aiden want to go? "Ibiza?"

"Ibiza was amazing and a constant party," Aiden said. He grinned. "But my favorite would have to be the Grand Canyon."

"The Grand Canyon?" I was a little surprised. I had expected a something flashy and full of excitement, not a giant hole in the ground.

"I liked the way it made me feel," he explained. His eyes went distant as he remembered. "All my problems were so small and inconsequential there. You can feel the eons there, and it just puts everything into perspective. Plus, the stars at night are absolutely breathtaking."

"I've never been there," I said with a shrug. "The pictures look amazing, though."

"The pictures don't do it justice." His hazel focus came back to me. "I'll take you there someday."

A flutter went through my stomach at the casual reference to us seeing one another after this trip.

"I'd like that," I replied honestly. "I really, really would."

He grinned and moved to kiss me. His kiss tasted faintly of mustard, but I still thought it was wonderful. I treasured that mustard kiss like it was gold.

"You'd have to find the time off from being a lawyer to come with me," he said when we broke apart. "I would want to show you all of it."

Cold ice settled in the pit of my stomach. Guilt threatened to overtake my happiness. "Oh, yeah. Right."

I knew I needed to tell him. I knew I should just blurt out the words, "I'm not a lawyer!" but nothing came out.

This was so perfect. He wanted to take me to his favorite place in the world. Telling him now would only ruin things. Plus, we were out on the middle of the ocean in a boat. I hated the idea of driving back in silence. It could wait until later.

He brushed hair from my face and back behind my ear. I loved that he did that. It made me feel cherished. "You are so beautiful."

I looked up, my guilt melted by the heat in his eyes. Want made his gaze burn and set my soul aflame. He kissed me again, this time slower and with more purpose. His tongue infused raw desire straight into my mouth. He reached for my shirt, lifting it easily up over my head.

I moaned his name against his kiss as the shirt cleared. "I thought we were fishing..." I murmured as his hands caressed the fabric of my swim top, my nipples hardening and responding to his touch.

He nibbled on my shoulder, sending heat straight down my spine and to my core. "I can stop if you want..."

"No, no, no... don't stop," I gasped as he put his mouth to the delicate skin of my neck and sucked. He smiled against my skin. I bit my lip and looked out across the water. There wasn't a soul for miles, but the idea of doing it out in broad daylight had a delicious naughtiness to it.

He released the tension of his kiss, causing my skin to sting. I hoped he hadn't left too much of a hickey, especially since I couldn't get away with wearing a turtleneck in the Caribbean. He blew on the now incredibly sensitive skin, chuckling as I shivered and goosebumps raced down my arms. It almost hurt when he kissed the spot again, trailing his tongue down the curve of my shoulder and distracting me while he untied my top.

My cute swimsuit fell away before I had a chance to

press it up. I didn't fight him as he untied the back string and left me completely exposed in front of him. We were alone out on the water and I had no reason to stop. Just the opposite, in fact.

His hand cupped my bare flesh and he instinctively groaned with pleasure. The sound of his want drove me wild. Unbearable need was heating my core like a furnace and only he could put out my flames. The fact that he was now using his fingers to turn my nipple into a hard pebble only fed the fire.

I shimmied out of my shorts and bottoms as he used both hands and mouth on me. He palmed and pinched while sucking and kissing my shoulders and neck. Aiden had found a spot just along my jaw line that was making my thighs moist.

The Caribbean sun was hot on my skin, but the cool breeze off the water made it tolerable. I decided that Aiden had far too many clothes on and that he should remove them in order to be as comfortable as I was. I grabbed his shirt, pulling it over his head. He didn't resist and moved his arms to help me, but never stopped touching and kissing.

His chest was all muscle under my hands. I pushed his shoulders hard, making him stumble back onto the bench. I loved the view of him looking up at me, hazel eyes wide and practically drooling as I straddled his hips. I smiled as I writhed my naked body against him. His swim trunks were struggling to contain his erection. Even through the fabric, he was hard and ready to take me.

His physical reaction was like a drug. It was visceral and stroked my ego that I could inspire this kind of desire. I loved that I turned him on. With that thought on my mind, my hips started to rock against his length.

In return, he pressed his mouth to my breast and began

to suck. Using teeth, tongue and suction, he drew the want straight from my core up my entire spine until I was undulating with need. Every flick of his tongue made me moan and writhe harder.

I couldn't stand it anymore. I could feel his cock pressing against my opening, begging for entrance and I wanted to give it to him. It was all I could think of. Every fiber in my body ached with desperate need to have him inside of me.

I reached down, moved his shorts to the side and took out his length. His hip arched in a primal response to my touch, searching out the way to complete me. I stroked him, feeling the blood rushing through and pulsating in my hand.

"I want you," I whispered, palming his hardness and feeling my insides contract with want.

"The basket," he groaned. "In the side pouch."

I kept one hand on him as I leaned back and searched the basket with the other. The condom square was easy to find.

"So sure you were going to get lucky, weren't you?" I teased, tearing open the package.

"I was certainly hoping for the best." His joking tone was betrayed by his wide pupils and the sheer desire painted in broad strokes across his face. "Never hurts to be prepared."

The corners of his lips tipped up in a smile, but there was obvious tension in his shoulders as he struggled to contain himself. He wanted me so badly he was practically shaking.

I slipped the condom down his hard length and then followed it with myself. His body reacted as soon as mine touched his. Arching his hips and grabbing my waist, he pushed himself to the hilt. He filled me so completely, so wonderfully, that I forgot to breathe. Luckily, my body knew what to do.

Aiden's eyes drifted shut and he tipped his head back with a groan as I started a slow grind. I held onto his solid shoulders and worked circles and arches, rocking and rolling my hips to have him touch every inch of my insides.

He gripped my hips to the point where I thought his fingers might leave bruises, but I didn't care. We were dancing the ageless dance of lovers. We matched our rhythm and movements, slowly pulling one another up the incline to climax.

My hair fell down my back as I arched my back, feeling the crescendo building between us. Looking down, our eyes met. They were more beautiful than the turquoise waters surrounding us. I dove into them, losing myself in his eyes as he lost himself in my body.

His pace intensified. Raw need blazed between us, threatening to overwhelm every sense. I matched him thrust for thrust, until I tipped over the edge into Aiden's oblivion. I heard my voice cry out in pleasure, but I didn't remember opening my mouth. For a long time, everything but Aiden spun out of control. I clung to him as pleasure racked both our bodies.

I collapsed forward, gasping for breath. Aiden wrapped his arms around me, holding me close as if he was still spinning out of control too. My mind took it's time returning to my body as I sat up. Aiden was smiling at me.

"Wow," I gasped, struggling to find my voice. It was hoarse from screaming I only vaguely remembered.

"I don't know how you do that to me," he whispered, touching my cheek with his fingers. "You are amazing."

Pride flushed my cheeks. "Thanks. You're pretty amazing yourself."

"Well, obviously," he responded as if I had said he had two eyes and a nose. "I'm the best there is."

"Cocky much?" I pushed his shoulders slightly. In response, he thrust his hips up to demonstrate his position of cockiness. It made me whimper with pleasure.

"It's not ego if it's true."

I had no comeback for that. As far as I was concerned, it was true. He was the best lover I had ever had. I knew that if I told him that though, he would go straight to his head, so instead I just kissed him.

I didn't want to break away from him, but nature was telling me it was inevitable. I pulled back, staying on his lap for just a moment longer. "Do we still get to fish today, or was this the whole purpose of the boat?" I asked, nodding to our location.

Aiden chuckled. "If this were the whole purpose, I would have gotten a comfier boat."

## CHAPTER 14

$\mathcal{I}$ sat on the edge of the boat, my feet dangling in the water and my head resting on Aiden's shoulder in complete bliss. I didn't care if we caught a single fish for the rest of the day-- I was having a fantastic time.

I could see a boat in the distance, but I didn't pay them much attention until it was clear they were headed straight for us. For a moment, I wondered if they had somehow heard my screams of pleasure and thought I needed rescuing.

The boat was slightly larger than ours, but with more storage and less speed. A man with aviator glasses and jet black hair was steering while a woman in a wetsuit gave him directions from the on-board computer. They silenced their engines to a throttle as they came alongside ours.

"I'm going to need to see your fishing licenses," the man asked. I didn't see any official emblems on their boat, but I supposed they could be with the coast guard. I hoped Aiden had the appropriate documentation needed.

"And I'm going to need to talk to your supervisor," Aiden retorted without looking up from his fishing line. I felt my eyes go wide at his flippant tone, but kept the rest of my face still. It certainly wasn't the tactic I would have used to get out of a ticket.

"Then you should probably stop by the facilities and see her sometime," the woman in the other boat replied. "I'm still trying to get in touch with your brother. We're booked out for months because of him, but he won't answer my calls."

"As much as I know Logan appreciates your interest, he's with Olivia now," Aiden said, grinning up at them. These people were obviously his friends. He changed his expression to look scandalized. "Besides, what would your husband think?"

"It would really just depend on what I would get in return. Olivia's pretty cute," the dark-haired man answered with a wink I could see over his sunglasses. The woman smacked his chest in pretend disgust at his sexualized comment.

"I wondered if we might run into you out here." Aiden laughed, rising to his feet. I mimicked his motion, but stayed quiet since I didn't know them. "Izzy can't stay away from me when I'm on a boat."

"Hey! That was a long time ago, and it was dark, and I thought you were Noah!" the woman exclaimed, rolling her eyes. She leaned up against the man next to her. He laughed and put his arm around her in solidarity. Love floated around the two of them in heavy waves.

"Now, Aiden..." The man tipped his sunglasses up onto his head, revealing spectacular blue eyes. He smiled at me. It was a breathtaking smile, but it didn't make me go weak in the knees the way Aiden's did. No, as amazing as this man's smile was, it was obviously meant for someone else. "At least your brother knows how to introduce a pretty girl to his friends."

Even though I wasn't interested in him, I still blushed at the compliment.

"Lena, this is Noah and his wife, Izzy," Aiden introduced. "Noah and I used to box together in college and Izzy runs a marine sanctuary on the island. The shark lab there is a big hit with the tourists."

"It's nice to meet you both," I said with a grin.

"It's a pleasure to meet you, too!" Izzy bubbled. "If you want to come by the sanctuary later, I'd be happy to give you a tour." I instinctively liked her friendly nature. She reminded me a lot of Darcie.

"Now, Lena," Noah said, his face serious. "You seem like a nice girl, so I have to ask what you're doing out here in this rust-bucket with this scoundrel."

"He kidnapped me," I answered, keeping my face as serious as possible. I was enjoying the easy, joking atmosphere the three of them had going on and wanted to join in. "Something about needing bait for sharks."

Izzy laughed. "It must be working. She's right under your boat."

"She?" Aiden asked, paling a little. "I'm not helping you catch this one. The last time I helped you, I nearly ended up an appetizer."

I glanced back and forth between the two of them, not quite following. I really hoped Izzy didn't mean that a shark was under our boat. Especially since I had just been splashing my feet in the water.

"Well, I didn't come out here just to see you, Aiden," Izzy teased. "But don't worry, I'm just tracking this shark, not trying to catch her. Besides, you were fine."

"I was in the ocean next to a very large shark," Aiden

countered. "I would prefer to keep my animal encounters to ones under me on the food chain."

"There's a shark under our boat?" I asked, peering over the edge of our suddenly very flimsy, floating vehicle. I was expecting to at least see a dark shape, but all I saw was dark blue water.

"A lemon shark, to be precise," Izzy answered. Her eyes lit up like a kid at Christmas. Noah smiled at her enthusiasm for the creature, love showing in his gaze.

The finale of the movie "Jaws" ran through my head. "Do we need to leave? I don't want to upset a shark." I didn't know what the proper procedure regarding sharks and boats was. There wasn't exactly a lot of shark education taught in landlocked states.

Izzy grinned and shook her head. "Oh no, you're fine. She doesn't care as long as you don't go down and try to pet her."

"That wasn't on my list of things to do today," I assured her. In fact, I was pretty sure my feet were staying up in the boat for the rest of our trip. "Why are you tracking her?"

"We just got some new tracking equipment and are testing it out." Izzy explained indicating to the computer on their dash. "Our girl here is pregnant, so as part of my research, I've been keeping a close eye on her."

I nodded, and looked over the side again. All I could think of was one of my dad's bad corny jokes.

*Why won't sharks attack lawyers? Professional courtesy.* Hardy har har.

Izzy started babbling on about her research and something about a reef and mangroves, but I was completely lost. Laws and statutes were my thing, not biology and experiments. I nodded politely, but Noah must have seen my glazed expression.

"Izzy, they don't need the taxonomical breakdown of the species," he said gently, putting a hand on her shoulder to curb the flow of shark related words.

"That's not even close to what I was talking about," she responded indignantly. Izzy glared up at him and then promptly looked a little bashful. She turned to Aiden. "I was going off into science mode again, wasn't I?"

"Just a little," Aiden answered. He held his hand up with his thumb and forefinger just inches apart.

"Sorry." She gave me a mortified smile. "I just get so excited about it I forget that not everyone is obsessed like I am."

I grinned at her. She was absolutely adorable. Noah gave her shoulder a gentle squeeze that showed he loved her more than any words could have explained. There was a love story wrapped around the two of them that I could just see the edges of. I knew it was something beautiful.

The computer beeped, and Izzy jumped excitedly to look at it.

"What are the two of you doing for dinner?" Noah asked while Izzy evaluated the screen. "I know Izzy would love to regale someone new with her shark tales this evening." Izzy turned and stuck her tongue out at him.

"I'm afraid we have plans," Aiden answered quickly. "Thank you, though."

I didn't know that the two of us had plans, but I stayed quiet and just smiled apologetically. I was very okay with having plans as long as they involved Aiden.

"That's too bad. Maybe next time?" Noah smiled, and I knew he legitimately meant it.

"That would be wonderful," I answered. I would love to meet some of Aiden's friends.

"She's heading west," Izzy said, pointing at the computer

screen. She looked up and smiled. "It was great to meet you, Lena. Aiden, tell your brother or Olivia to call me. I can't keep up with the business they've been sending our way. I mean, it's great, but I'm going to have to hire someone if they keep it up."

"I'll make sure he gets the message," Aiden assured her. "It's good to see you two."

Noah started up his boat's engine and waved as they pulled away to follow Izzy's shark. We watched them for a moment.

"So what are our dinner plans?" I asked, turning to Aiden once the boat was out of hearing.

"I was thinking room service." Aiden gave me the cocky smile that made my knees go weak and my willpower disappear.

"Oh, that sounds nice," I replied a little breathless. "I can see why you wouldn't want to invite them."

"Yes." Aiden ran his finger along my collarbone, pausing to gently stroke the fading red mark he had left earlier with his lips. "That and the fact that Izzy never stops talking about her sharks. Ever."

## CHAPTER 15

*L*aying out on a blanket with Aiden on the beach, my throat was sore from laughing so hard. I stared up at the night sky and wished on every star up there that we would always be this happy. Aiden made me laugh without even trying, and when he did try, I was completely unable to stop. He had quickly discovered that I would snort if I laughed hard enough, which he thought was hilarious. He then, of course made it his mission in life to make me snort.

I hated snorting, but I loved how hard it made Aiden laugh when I did. Once he started laughing at my snort, I would laugh even harder, causing me to snort again, and the two of us would be lost to an unending laughing loop until we couldn't breathe. My ribs ached and my face was sore, but I had never been so happy in my entire life.

The remnants of our dinner sat back on my porch, and we were now enjoying an evening of whispering under the stars. Aiden had selected a fabulous bottle of white wine for the two of us, and I had lost track of the time completely as the two of us lay side by side watching the galaxy spin by.

Our conversation had started out as a simple question, followed by another, which we quickly turned into a game. The rules were simple. Ask any question and the other had to answer it without going off topic. We'd been at it for hours, but I wanted to know everything about him.

"Okay, my turn," I said, reaching for the open bottle of wine in Aiden's hand. He handed to me and I sipped directly out of the bottle. "Favorite junk food."

"French fries," Aiden instantly answered.

"Any specific brand? Or are you a french fry snob?"

"Any kind." He turned his face to me in the darkness and I could just make out the outline of his smile in the dark. "I probably shouldn't tell you this, but french fries are my kryptonite."

"I'll keep that in mind the next time I need to trap you so you don't foil my evil plots," I teased, taking another sip of wine. It was going straight to my head and making me deliciously tipsy.

"Ah, but then I'd just eat my way to freedom," he countered. I laughed, imagining a fence made out for french fries keeping Aiden pinned until he gnawed his way out.

"My turn," Aiden said, taking the bottle from me. "How did you know you wanted to be a lawyer?"

"My sister," I answered. I didn't even have to think on that one. It was in the essay I was writing for my application.

"Go on," he encouraged, taking a sip for himself. "I'm curious to know why you would choose a career known to be evil."

I stuck my tongue out at him and said the first thing that popped in my head. "You're evil."

He laughed and handed me the bottle. "This is true. Have some more wine and tell me why you want to join the dark side."

I shook my head and took the bottle.

"My little sister wasn't an easy child. She was always pushing the envelope on what she could get away with. I'm her big sister, so I'm supposed to look out for her, protect her." I explained. "As a kid, I took that to mean I should get her out of trouble. I would go in front of my parents and present arguments and evidence showing how the broken lamp was an accident or that the dog really did look better with the haircut. It was my dream ever since."

Aiden kissed my temple. "You sound like a good big sister. That's the best reason I've heard to be a lawyer."

A good big sister, maybe, but I certainly wasn't a lawyer. Guilt weighed heavy on my conscience. I had been very careful not to say I was a lawyer, but I never said I wasn't one either. I tried to convince myself that I wasn't lying to him because he had never actually asked if I was a lawyer, but I wasn't having much success. I felt like a liar. A big, fat one. A lie of omission was still a lie, but...

If I told him, he would know that I had been keeping it a secret for the past few days. That I had completely lied about winning a case when I first met him. I knew I should have just told him the very first day on the island. He would have completely understood then. If I told him now, I would ruin the evening, and possibly the rest of the vacation.

I looked over at his silhouette in the dark. I didn't want to lie to him. I wanted to tell him everything about myself and for him to tell me everything about him. My alcohol infused brain said to go for it. What was the worst that could happen?

"Aiden, I need to tell you something." I took a big sip of wine for courage. If I told him now and he hated me for it, I was pretty sure I could deal with it. I would survive. I was falling head over heels in love with him, but at least neither one of us had said anything permanent yet.

"That's not how you play the game," he chided. "It's your turn to ask a question, not to give an answer."

I bit my lip, torn. The strength to tell him was quickly ebbing. Everything was so perfect. I didn't want to ruin it. I sighed. Telling him could wait. I still had half the trip left before we had to go back to real life. He didn't need to know yet. He would understand.

"Fine. I'll tell you later. It's important, though." I took another swig of wine to wash down the guilt. *I will tell him*, I promised myself. I just needed to find a better time to do so. The right time. For now, I would just enjoy finding out more about him. "What do you want most in the world?"

"French fries."

I gave his shoulder a playful push. "Real answers, remember?"

He stared up at the sky, his eyes searching for something that wasn't there. "I want to find my place in the world," he said after a moment. "I've lived in my father's shadow for so long that I don't know how to escape it, or even if I want to. I want to make him proud, but..."

I snuggled into his shoulder, trying to give him some comfort. I wanted to take some of his pain away.

He sighed. "I never seem to be enough for him. For anyone, really."

"You're more than enough, Aiden," I informed him. "If he can't see how wonderful you are, then he doesn't deserve you."

"What makes you think I'm so wonderful? You barely know me."

His words stung. He was right. I hadn't even spent a full week with him yet, but something inside of me knew better.

"I met you three weeks ago and you changed my life. You weren't even trying to, but you gave me courage. You believed in me after thirty seconds."

*"You won't be lower level for long,"* he remembered. "I guess I was right. But, Lena-"

I cut him off before he could tell me that he hadn't meant it. I knew he had. "That night, I was able to go in front of my boss and show what I could do because someone had told me I could. I know that it didn't matter much to you, but it mattered to me. If you have that kind of effect on me, then you have it with everyone you meet."

"That doesn't mean I'm wonderful. There's things you don't know about me," he said darkly.

I sat up, placed the bottle in the sand, and looked down at him. "I know enough. If you want me to know more, then tell me."

He looked up at me, his eyes reflecting the cold, distant starlight. "You sure? I could be a very different person than the one you think you know. How do you know that I'm not a terrible person?"

"Because of this." I leaned down and kissed him. His lips were soft and tender, and full of desire. There was strength and sweetness. It was all about emotion and the gut reaction his kiss gave me every time. I didn't care if this was a fling or real. Everything a girl could ever want in a kiss was in his lips. "When you kiss me, I know all I need to."

He was quiet for a moment. I knew it was silly for me to have these feeling for him so quickly, but I didn't care. My heart and my gut said that he was a good person, that he was everything I wanted in a man. For once, I was listening with my heart instead of my brain, and my heart said he was what I wanted.

"In that case, I should kiss you all the time." He was back

to his usual self, confident and charming. He patted his shoulder for me to retake my place. I only paused for a moment before cuddling back into him.

"I wouldn't complain one bit," I said as he wrapped his arm around me. "You can kiss me anytime you want."

I liked the way he felt beneath me, but something now felt off. My brain wasn't quite as willing to stay silent to the confidence of my heart. I wondered what he meant by his words, "I could be a very different person than the one you think you know." If I had a secret I hadn't told him, it was very possible that he had some he hadn't revealed to me. I wondered what Aiden the Assistant could be hiding.

"Okay, my turn," Aiden announced. "How many boyfriends have you had?"

"You really want to know?" I could feel my cheeks heating and I was glad we were in the dark.

"Yes, I need to know who my competition is."

"Four serious ones." I sighed, knowing he would want more information than that. "The last serious one being a little over a year ago. I've been on a couple of dates since, but nothing really has clicked. You don't have any competition."

"Of course I do," Aiden replied. "You're a beautiful woman. Any man who sees you is my competition."

I smiled. The sentiment was slightly chauvinistic, but it was still sweet. "When was your last serious relationship?" I asked.

"Give me some of that wine." He sighed, holding out his hand.

"That bad, huh?" I teased. He took a moment to answer.

"I'm good with women. I know what women want and how to get them to give me what I want." He said it as fact, rather than boasting. Given his good looks and charm, I could believe it. "But, I'm not good at relationships."

"That's not what I asked," I said after a moment of quiet. My brain started to whisper that my heart might not like the answer to this particular question after all.

He sighed. "The last real relationship I had was in college. I thought it was love, but..." He shook his head and took a big swig of wine. "I haven't had a serious relationship since. Plenty of non-serious ones, but nothing that ever mattered. Ben says I have trust issues when it comes to women. That I don't let them stay in my life."

"Is Ben right?" I held my breath, afraid of his response.

"That's two questions, but I'll answer it," he replied after a moment. "Ben's always right. It's part of why I trust him so much."

I kept the hurt growing in my chest inside. Aiden wasn't ready for a serious relationship. I silently chided myself for even thinking for a moment that this relationship would continue the moment we stepped off the island. I was just his latest fling.

I looked up at the stars and blinked away the blurriness. I could handle this. If this thing with Aiden was a fling, it would make it that much easier to go back to real life. I could stop myself from falling in love with him now, before I grew too attached. I wouldn't have to tell him I wasn't a lawyer because this would be over as soon as we left the island.

"Do you want to know what Ben thinks about you?" Aiden asked, his voice clear in the dark.

"Is that your question this turn?" I countered. I was glad my voice didn't shake. "If it's not, then I don't want to answer."

Aiden shifted on the sand beside me, rolling onto his side so he could look at me. I stared up at the sky. If I looked at him, I knew my face would give me away. This was just a good time to him.

"Ben says you're the real deal." I could feel him watching me. "He likes you. He says you're good for me."

I didn't say anything. My heart was so confused I didn't know what *to* say. Aiden didn't do relationships, but his boss thought I was good for him. Apparently, this amazing thing I had going with Aiden was just a fling, but then Ben's words gave me the illusion of hope.

I felt Aiden return to laying on his back beside me. Just our shoulders touched and I ached for more. I wanted him, fling or not. I wasn't sure the true depth of what I felt yet, but I knew I definitely felt something.

I didn't know how this vacation was going to end. I wanted to believe it would be a fairy tale, that Aiden and I would go back to Chicago and live happily ever after. But Aiden wasn't a prince and I wasn't Cinderella. There was a very real chance that we would never see each other again once this dream of a vacation ended.

I tried to tell myself that I was okay with that, but deep down I knew I wasn't. I already felt things for Aiden that I didn't want to give up. I liked the way he made me feel. I like who I was when I was with him. I didn't want to go back to my old life and go back to what I had been.

I took his hand in mine and squeezed, pushing my uneasy thoughts to the side. Tonight, I would share whatever secrets Aiden asked of me. I would accept that this was just a short term thing and do my best to enjoy it.

"It's my turn," Aiden said, taking the bottle from its spot in the sand. "Tell me about your first kiss."

"You're going to laugh. It was pretty terrible," I warned him.

"I sincerely doubt that," Aiden replied, pulling me to rest on his shoulder. "Kissing you is never terrible."

I nestled into the hollow of his shoulder, soaking up the feeling of his arm around me and the smell of his skin. If this did have to end at the end of my trip, at least I would have some amazing memories.

## CHAPTER 16

"*V*acation agrees with you," Kathryn commented, startling me out of me out of my day dreams.

"What?" I could feel a blush blaze across my cheeks and I wondered if she could read my thoughts. They were certainly blush-worthy.

"You've been staring off at the water with a happy smile plastered on your face for the entire meeting," she informed me.

"Sorry. Did I miss something important?" I couldn't even remember what the meeting was about. "I wasn't sure if I got the projector set up properly--"

"Everything was fine," she assured me, with a smile. "I'm just stating that you look very happy. That assistant must be very good for you."

I relaxed and grinned. "He is." She had no idea just how good. He was beyond good.

"I'm guessing you have dinner plans tonight, then," Kathryn said with a knowing smile.

I starting packing up the laptop and notes from the

meeting. "Not if you need me. You brought me here, so you have dibs on me."

Kathryn laughed and shook her head. "I don't need you tonight. I'm just meeting a couple of old school friends and thought I'd invite you to tag along so you wouldn't be bored."

I stopped and bit my lip. Aiden was taking me out to dinner, but Kathryn might know someone who had some pull with the law school.

"You should go keep adding to your happy glow," Kathryn told me, seeing my hesitation. "We're going to just be reliving old times. And none of them are on the school board, so unless you are planning on changing firms, they won't get you far. I just didn't want you to spend the whole trip by yourself."

I smiled gratefully as I put the last few things from the meeting away. It was almost unnerving how easily Kathryn could read me. "Thanks. How'd you know what I was thinking?"

"I was there once and remember how desperate I was to follow my dreams." She held open the conference room door for me. "Just make sure you're ready for the meeting tomorrow. I'll actually need you to take notes next time."

"Yes, ma'am," I promised, turning off the light before leaving the room. "I'll be there and ready."

Kathryn started down the path in the opposite direction of me, but she paused and looked over her shoulder. "Have fun tonight," she said with a wink. It was very clear she knew exactly what kind of fun she was expecting me to have. I blushed a deep crimson, but she had already turned around and started walking.

I watched her for a moment before turning and heading to my room to put the laptop away for the day. Grinning, I walked faster, already imagining just how good the night was going to be. I clutched the laptop bag to my chest, closing my eyes and feeling the warm sunshine as I thought about Aiden. There was nothing in the world that could ruin this trip.

HAPPINESS. I embodied the word. Aiden's hand was warm in mine, holding me close to him. Golden sunlight glinted off the curls of his hair and glimmered in the green and brown depths of his eyes. He walked through the resort as if he owned the place, all calm confidence and charisma. I walked proudly beside him, knowing that every female who saw him wanted to be in my shoes.

He glanced over at me, smiling at what he saw. I blushed, feeling beautiful in his gaze. The way he looked at me made my heart flutter and the space between my legs heat. I loved the way his shirt displayed his broad shoulders and tapered to his narrow waist. He managed to look sexy just walking down the street. If there hadn't been people around, I would have pinned him to a palm tree and had my way with him.

He tugged gently on my hand, pulling me away from the restaurant and toward the beach instead. My light skirt caught the gentle breeze off the ocean and fluttered slightly, threatening to expose me, but I followed him willingly. Ben sat at a small table overlooking the beach reading a newspaper. I nodded respectfully as we passed, earning a slight head bob from him. Aiden ignored him completely.

"Where are we going?" I asked as we stepped off the path and onto the sand. I was glad I had chosen sensible but cute flats as shoes. I didn't have to take them off as long as I didn't kick up too much sand. "I thought we were going to dinner."

"We are," he promised, grinning with a secret. His eyes caught the warmth of the tropical sun and sparkled. "Dinner is on the beach.

I beamed back at him as we made our way down the beach. I could see a beautiful white gazebo with a table and chairs waiting for us next to the water. Candles flickered on the table and a bottle of wine stood waiting for our arrival. It was like something out of a magazine.

Aiden hurried over to pull out my chair, holding it for me and even handing me my napkin once I was seated. Chivalry wasn't dead, apparently.

"Wine?" he asked, motioning to the bottle waiting in an ice bucket.

"Yes, please," I replied eagerly. I wondered just what kind of new wine experience he had planned for me this time.

He uncorked it with ease, handing me the cork as he poured a small amount into a glass. He moved so gracefully, I barely registered the feel of the cork or even the smell because I was entranced by him. He caught me watching and smiled. A delightful warmth settled in the pit of my stomach that was better than any wine.

I picked up the glass of wine and swirled, watching the clear liquid inside. It was a white with legs similar to the wine I had the last time. "It smells sweet, like peaches."

He nodded, pleased with his pupil. "Try it."

I closed my eyes and took a small sip, letting the flavors coat my tongue. "It's bubbly and sweet like grape juice. There's no bite at the end at all-- it's almost like drinking candy."

"Do you like it?" Even without opening my eyes, I could

feel his hopeful gaze upon me. He had chosen this wine specifically for me.

"I love it." I opened my eyes, smiling as I dove into his. "What is it?"

He smiled wide, proud of choosing something I liked. "It's a moscato from Australia. I thought you might like it. It's sweet like you."

"You thought right," I said, taking a second, larger sip before handing him my glass for more. He filled my glass as well as his before sitting. Everything was beautiful. The white gauzy fabric of the gazebo floated lazily on the soft breeze, far from the gentle flicker of the candle flames. The ocean provided the background music, a soft murmur punctuated with cries from seagulls in the distance. "This is amazing, by the way. Thank you."

"You deserve it," he stated, sipping on his wine and looking very pleased with himself. He had certainly outdone every expectation I could have ever had for a romantic dinner, and the food hadn't even come out yet.

"Aiden..." I bit my lip as he looked up at me. I felt terrible complaining about such a wonderful gift like this, but it was too much. This couldn't have been cheap, especially on an assistant's salary. I had to say something. Maybe if we left early he could get a portion of his money back. "You really didn't have to do this. I mean, it's fantastic and beautiful, but it's too much."

"Is there something wrong with it?" He frowned, glancing at the ornate silverware and candles. "There was an option for an indoor version, but-"

"No, there's nothing wrong with it," I cut him off. "It's just that this couldn't have been covered by the all-inclusive part of this resort. I don't know what you paid, but it was too much just to impress me. You've already impressed me."

Aiden stared at me for a moment as if I were speaking a foreign language and then started to laugh. "Lena, you're amazing."

I opened my mouth, but I couldn't find anything to say. I was certainly not expecting to be called amazing for telling him that he didn't need to spend this much on me. "How in the world does me telling you that make me amazing?"

"Please don't worry about the cost. It's all comped. One of the benefits of working where I do." He reached out and took my hands in his. I narrowed my eyes, trying to determine if he was telling me the truth. It sounded possible, but this was still way too expensive for the likes of me. "You are amazing because you are concerned about my well being. Most of the girls I've dated would want to know why there weren't roses on the table as well."

"It's just so much," I said, looking around at the extravagance. I could only imagine what the resort was going to cook up for us as far as food. "If they don't think this is too much, then you've been dating the wrong kind of girls."

"I most certainly have," was all Aiden said. I wanted to ask him more, but he smiled and squeezed my hands. "You deserve this."

I wasn't sure I did, but he obviously had his mind made up about it. I would just sit back, enjoy it, and order the cheapest thing on the menu. Just because it was going to be comped didn't mean I needed to take advantage.

A waiter cleared his throat gently to gain our attention. With a polite nod of his head, he placed a plate of cheeses on the table. "I hope the two of you are hungry," he said with a thick island accent. "The chef has prepared his best for the two of you."

I grinned at Aiden, reaching for a piece of cheese. I had never had the chef prepare me something special, but then I had never had dinner on a beach with candlelight either. The waiter murmured something about getting more wine before hurrying away to leave us alone with the cheese.

I nibbled on a soft white cheese I was pretty sure was the best brie I'd ever tasted. The wine complimented every bite, bringing out new flavors and highlighting the original ones. I felt very rich and spoiled, munching on fancy cheese and sipping wine as the orange sun hung heavy on the edge of the horizon with dark, gray clouds filling the sky for contrast.

Aiden cleared his throat. He fiddled with the stem of his wineglass for a moment in an uncharacteristic display of nerves. "Lena, I was hoping I could ask you a favor."

"Is that what all this is for?" I asked, indicating the fancy spread before us.

"No, though I hope it helps you decide to say yes." A quick grin flashed across his face.

"Okay." I nodded. "I will certainly take it into consideration."

Aiden took a sip of his wine and carefully set the glass down before speaking. "My brother is getting married in two weeks. I need a date for the wedding."

I couldn't stop the grin from filling my face, but I managed to keep it under control. "And you need me to introduce you to someone. I think my roommate has a couple of weekends open..."

His hazel eyes opened in surprise when I didn't immediately say yes, then crinkled at the corners as he realized what I was up to. "Lena, I don't want your roommate."

I knew this was a big deal. It would mean meeting not only his brother, but his father as well. It meant that he thought I was worthy to present to them. My heart was full to bursting that he thought that highly of me, but I wanted him to ask me directly. I needed him to after the conversation we had last night. "Well, I might have a co-worker who I could set you up with."

"I don't want your roommate, or your co-worker, or even your dog groomer." He smiled, knowing that I was just messing with him. He stood and came to kneel by my chair. "Would you please be my date to my brother's wedding?"

I grinned at him. "Yes. I would be honored to."

"You had to be difficult, didn't you?" he asked. I nodded and he leaned forward and kissed me, putting his hand in my hair and pulling me into him. Happiness washed over me like a wave. This was going to be more than just a vacation fling.

"This has been the best trip of my life," I whispered, my words coming straight from my heart. There was a chance for us. "I'm so glad I met you."

He grinned. "You sure it's not just because I got you some amazing cheese?"

I pretended to think on it for a minute as he walked back to his chair. "Nope. It's all you."

"Good." He popped a cracker into his mouth and winked. "But it did help, right?"

I laughed. "You got me. I'm actually part mouse. I probably should have told you earlier."

"That does explain the tail..."

I threw a piece of cheese at his head. It missed by a mile, but he still ducked.

His eyes met mine and I couldn't look away. They absorbed me. "Do you believe in fate?" he asked. His eyes were so beautiful I almost hated when he blinked.

"Yes," I said with a nod. "I do."

"Then you don't believe in free will?" He took a small sip of wine, waiting to see my reaction.

"I believe in both," I stated. He raised his eyebrows, the gentle merriment in his eyes telling me that he was genuinely interested in my thoughts. Not only was the man good with wine, but he apparently enjoyed philosophical discussions as well.

"How does that work?" Aiden asked, taking a piece of cheese for himself.

"I believe that fate pushes in the direction we're supposed to go, but we have to chose how to go there. We get to choose the path that leads us to our fate."

"Interesting," he said, slowly digesting my words. "What if I don't like my fate? Do I get to choose a different one?"

"No," I replied shaking my head. "We don't get to chose our fates, just how we accept them. Fate is that the sun is going to set and we will be in the dark. There is nothing we can do to stop it. It is what is destined to happen. But we have free will, so even though the sun sets and there is darkness, we can chose to gather and light candles."

Aiden munched quietly on his cheese for a moment as he contemplated my words. "So is it fate that I found you?"

"I'd like to think so." Happy excitement at revealing my feelings flutters in my chest. "I kind of like the idea that the universe is smiling on the two of us being together. What about you? Do you believe it was fate?"

Aiden sipped his wine thoughtfully, his hazel eyes dark with thought. Slowly, he set his glass down and leaned forward as if he were telling me a secret. "Up until a little under three weeks ago, I used to believe that fate was a word that the hopeless used to describe random chance. That fate was just a coward's way of hoping for the future or explaining the past. It didn't have any substance or meaning."

"What happened three weeks ago that changed your mind?"

Aiden's face brightened into a soft smile, one that was meant only for me. It was the kind of smile that made my heart race and my stomach do cartwheels. It was a smile that made it impossible for me to think of anything but Aiden and how much I cared for him.

"You. You happened," he answered. My heart fluttered harder. "The odds are astronomical that I would meet you. I've been in that office dozens of times, and I've never gotten lost..." He held up fingers as he began to count the obstacles.

"You've never come down to the Dungeons of the firm, have you?" I interjected.

"You mean the fifteenth floor? No, I guess not. I've never had reason to before this meeting. Add that to the list." He raised a second finger. "Throw in that it happened to be the day you were working late, that yours was the first office I found, and that you had such opportunity to show your strength."

"My strength?" I shot him a dubious look. "That was one of the worst days I've ever had. It was a terrible, terrible day that you actually made better. I didn't feel strong at all."

"You could have fooled me," he said, dropping his counting hand back to the table. He smiled, lighting up his face. "I've never connected with anyone the way I do with you. You make me laugh without trying and I can talk to you for hours. Not to mention you're pretty damn good in the sack."

I laughed. Leave it to a guy to bring sex into a romantic conversation.

"I always thought finding someone like you was just a product of random chance." He shook his head, and his honey hair caught the wind. "But that day was so perfectly orchestrated to avoid all the random chance, that it had to be fate. I had a better chance of winning the lottery than I did for all the necessary steps to meet you to happen."

"And then now we're having a romantic dinner in the Caribbean," I added. "That's pretty damn lucky."

"Not lucky," Aiden replied. "Fate."

I raised my wine glass. "To fate. To finding the person who completes us."

Aiden tipped his glass to mine and the air rang with a the chime of our glasses. "To fate."

As if on cue, thunder followed the chime. The wind picked at the tablecloth and started to make the gauzy gazebo quiver. A raindrop splattered on the sand behind me. The splooshing sound was loud enough to make me turn and see the storm that had silently crept up on our dinner.

Big drops of rain started to spot the ground like a work of modern art. Aiden and I looked at one another. He shrugged and reached for the bottle of wine as I blew out the candles. Taking my hand in his, we hurried from the gazebo toward the shelter of the resort.

Thunder boomed across the ocean, rumbling and shaking the entire island with is strength. The rain fell in sheets and we were both soaked long before we even cleared the sand. Lightning flickered and danced across the inky sky as we stumbled through the buildings to Aiden's room.

Aiden handed me the bottle of wine while he searched his pockets for his room key. I leaned against the wall, protected by the roof overhang from the rain. The storm was pouring buckets of water, but it was warm. I was soaked to the bone with it. Just the thirty second run from the beach had completely drenched the two of us.

Aiden's shirt was plastered to him like a second skin, showing every muscle and contour of his back and arms.

His light cotton pants were doing the same thing, hugging his perfect ass. Just looking at him, his hair dripping into his eyes as he opened the door made my mouth water.

"What?" he asked, catching me staring. "Do I have something in my teeth?"

I shook my head slowly. "Nope."

"Then, what?" He ran his hand through his hair, spraying raindrops across the porch. The rain had washed out his hair and now the natural curl was breaking free. It was just the kind of hair that was meant for tangling fingers in and my stomach clenched with want just thinking about what we would be doing to get there.

I pushed my body from the wall and directly into his arms. His mouth was a magnet for mine. I could taste the rain on his lips as I pressed my wet body against his. Even though the rain was warm, his body heat felt amazing next to mine. I ran my fingers through the damp curls on the back of his neck, loving the way it made him kiss me even harder.

"Wow," he whispered. My fingers were still playing with his hair. "I think I'll be having dessert first."

I grinned and he pushed a tendril of waterlogged hair from my face, tucking it behind my ear. I wanted to drown in his eyes when he looked at me like that. It was a look of pure want and desire with just enough heart to know he was mine.

He kissed me again, pushing the door open and guiding me through it. The room was dark, but the windows were open and the lightning was enough light to make it to the bedroom. He peeled his shirt off as we stumbled across the slippery wooden floors.

I drank in his kisses, enjoying every taste. Even though we were moving through his room, I still closed my eyes and focused on the taste of his lips. I assumed that he was pushing me to his bed, and I would have been eager to go there, but after a moment I realized we had been walking too long.

When a light switch flicked on, my eyes opened. We were standing in his bathroom. When I shot him a quizzical look, he shrugged. "We're all wet. I don't want us to get all cold and uncomfortable."

I laughed. "So, what do you suggest? Do you have a blow dryer in here?"

He broke away from my embrace, and I longed to feel him again. He reached in the cabinet under the sink. "I thought a shower might be nice, but..." With that, he pulled out a hair dryer. "We can do it this way instead."

I laughed. "I'll take the shower."

He grinned and started the water up. I reached around him and began to undo those white cotton pants while he checked the water temperature. As his pants started to come down, I grabbed his underwear and pulled those down as well. His ass was taut and muscular, and as he bent over to check the water temperature, I spanked him. It was a light spanking, but it was kind of out of character for me.

He looked back at me, one eyebrow cocked. I smiled and looked sheepish. He turned around, still trapped by his pants and underwear around his feet. He leaned in for a kiss, but at the last moment, his lips went to my ear instead. "Was it fate that caused you to spank me, or was it free will?"

I practically hummed with pleasure in his ear. "I wanted to spank you." It was definitely the truth.

He moved his lips down from my ear to my neck, and I could feel his fingers pulling at the bottom of my shirt. He pulled upward and I raised my arms to get it off quicker, revealing the lacy bra I was wearing. As soon as it was out of the way, he let it fall to the floor and leaned back in to kiss me. His hands were all over my body now, touching my ass through my skirt, running up my spine, and caressing my skin.

After a few moments, he moved his fingers to my bra. I felt him begin to struggle, and then his tongue stopped moving in my mouth. I laughed inwardly at how every man seemed to have a problem with this.

"I swear this only happens with you," he said, looking a little flustered.

I smiled, then moved my own hands behind myself to unclasp the bra. I did it quickly, and let the bra fall to the floor. His eyes dilated as he drank in the sight of my body.

"So, was that fate, or was it free will?" I asked, a mocking smile on my face.

"If it was fate, the universe is having a laugh at my expense right now," he said, leaning in for another kiss.

The steam was starting to fog up the room, so I backed away from him. I worked my skirt down and stepped out of it. "We should get in the shower," I said.

"Yes, we should!" he said with a little too much enthusiasm. I chuckled and began to put my hair up. I cursed for a moment when I realized I hadn't brought any hair bands with me. I began looking around the bathroom for something to tie my hair up.

"What's the matter?" Aiden asked.

"My hair. I wanted to tie it up so that it wouldn't get wet, or at least any wetter than it already is."

He looked a little crestfallen. "Really? Because I was kind of hoping to wash it."

"You want to wash my hair?"

He shrugged. "I want to do a lot of things to you, but I really love your hair."

It sounded sweet and innocent, and just looking at that naked man in front of me was enough to get me to nod my head. Even as small as the nod was, I saw his already hardening cock twitch a little. He was looking forward to it.

He jumped in the water, keeping the curtain pulled back for me. I watched him for a moment as he let the water run over his hair. He opened his eyes and looked at me, probably enjoying the same sight. "Coming?"

I grinned and stepped in. The water was hot, not scalding but it definitely sent a rush through my body when contrasted with the cold rainwater. I gasped a little, but Aiden wasted no time. He reached his hands around my waist and moved in, kissing me deeply.

I enjoyed the kiss as water fell on both of our heads. His hands quested all over my body, as if searching for a handhold, like he couldn't get enough of touching me. I could feel his hardness, now fully erect, against my belly. I wanted him so badly it hurt.

When his hands grasped my hair, I heard him inhale sharply. He clenched his fist, pulling it slightly. It made me weak in the knees, and I knew he felt me tremble. I was paralyzed as he worked his kisses down my neck.

His hand still in my hair, he slowly turned my head. My body turned with it, turning my back to him. I thought that he was overcome by lust, that he was going to take me right there. I was so ready, I wanted him *so bad*.

I felt his cock press against my ass, and I lifted myself up to my tiptoes so that he could enter more easily. I knew I was dripping wet, that he'd slide right into me. He let go of my hair, and I braced myself against the wall for what I thought was coming next.

I felt both his hands back in my hair, this time covered in shampoo. It felt *so* good. I could feel his fingers running through my hair, lathering up every inch of it, every strand. I heard him smell it, felt his breath on my ear as he exhaled, and every bit of it made me want him more.

I reached back and tried to find his cock. When I grasped it, I began to slide back and forth. He moved his hand to mine and gently guided it away. His lips went to my ear, and he whispered, "Just enjoy this."

*I can do that*, I thought with a smile.

One of his hands strayed from my hair and reached around me, cupping my breasts. I flattened my back against his muscular chest as he began to thrust against me. I could hardly call this dry humping, we were sopping wet. I felt the shampoo rinse from my hair, and I could feel myself dripping with desire. Every action he took drove me closer and closer to madness.

"Aiden," I moaned.

"Hmm?"

"I need you. I need you in me," I begged.

"I don't have a condom in here," he said slowly.

I smiled, but didn't turn around. "Don't worry about it. I'm on the pill. Besides," I trailed off, then looked back behind me. "I trust you."

I practically heard him growl behind me. This time, when his hands moved to my ass cheeks, I knew what he was going for. I got up on my tiptoes again, and I felt as he pressed against my opening. My body accepted him without hesitation. I felt him shudder as I enveloped him. He didn't stop until he was all the way in. He let his hands go to my hips, and I felt him begin to thrust against me.

I put my hands behind me, touching his face and neck while he began to increase his tempo, spreading me open more and more. His huge rod was skewering me, causing me to moan involuntarily. His hands on my hips let me know exactly who was in charge, and I let him use my body.

Suddenly, he pulled out of me, turned me around, and gave me a deep kiss. I kissed back, pressing myself against him. His hand lifted my leg up, placing my foot on the side of the tub. I wrapped my arms around the back of his neck as he pushed back into me.

One hand remained on my leg and the other wrapped around my waist as he writhed against me, and my nails found the skin of his back as I felt myself rising toward orgasm.

As if that weren't enough, he backed away, one hand going to the back of my neck as he continued to furiously pound into me. Our eyes locked, and he had a serious look on his face. It was the look of an animal, a slave to his own lust. Those hazel eyes bore into my soul, and I knew that being filled like this was going to drive me over the edge soon. Those eyes never left mine, not even when I felt my leg muscle begin to twitch under his grasp, not even when my jaw dropped in a wordless scream, not even when I felt my own eyes roll back into my head.

As the water poured over my body, I felt nothing but his manhood inside of me, hitting that spot over and over again. The rest of the world seemed to fade away as my orgasm hit, causing my whole body to twitch and shake. I could feel my leg muscle spasm, and still he kept hammering away at me. Wave after wave of pleasure hit me, turning my body to jelly.

I recovered just long enough to catch Aiden's face as he appeared deep in concentration. His eyes were no long locked with mine, instead they were staring at my tits. He had wrapped his arm around the other side of my leg, getting better leverage so that he could go even deeper. I saw his tongue dart out of his mouth for a moment, and his thrusting took on an even more frantic rhythm.

I knew where he was at, and in another moment he looked up at me. He looked almost pained, like he wanted to ask a question, but was unable to in his current state. I knew the question that he wanted to ask. He needed reassurance that what he wanted to do was okay, and I let him know exactly how I felt.

"Oh, yes, Aiden! Come for me," I cried out. I continued to moan loudly as he redoubled his efforts. He faced directly down, watching himself pump in and out of my body.\

I heard what sounded like an animal roar through gritted teeth as I felt a warm splash inside of me. I braced myself against the wall of the shower as another orgasm rocked through my body. Suddenly, he grabbed my hair and pulled my face down. Our eyes locked again as he continued to thrust within me with determination. I contracted on him over and over, the only movement I was able to make in this paralyzed state. It was so incredibly sexy.

He pulled out of me, the water already rinsing my fluids off of him. I knew that a bit of that sheen on him was sweat and not just shower water, and that was super hot too. He was breathing hard and his face was a little red, and I knew that I must look pretty similar at this point.

After a few more moments of silence, he looked up at me. "Wow," was all he had to say.

"Wow, indeed," I repeated back with a smile.

"It must have been fate that brought us together, because I don't think I could find another woman like you." He said it so casually that I knew it was the truth, but it stirred something deep inside me.

He must have seen me getting emotional, so he leaned

in and gave me a hug. I loved his hugs, especially in this warm shower.

He broke away from me. "You want to eat the rest of that dinner?"

"Sure," I said. I opened the door of the shower and hopped out. Suddenly, I felt a sharp SMACK against my ass. I squealed and looked back, shocked at what he had done.

He wore a cocky grin. "Can't decide if that one was fate or free will."

## CHAPTER 17

*A*iden snored gently and I found myself loving the sound. The rain had stopped some time in the night, but Aiden's soft noises were even better than the gentle patter of water. His hair was splayed across the pillow, and his mouth was slightly open. He looked so peaceful and utterly content. I slept better with him than I ever did alone, and waking up next to him made mornings bearable. A girl could certainly get used to a naked man in her bed like Aiden.

I leaned over and kissed his cheek. He mumbled something about "just five more minutes" before twisting under the blankets and hiding away from the sun. I couldn't help but smile as I went to the door to find my shoes.

I had to get ready for Kathryn's meeting, and as the only clothing I had was my still damp outfit from the night before, I had to leave early in order to change and prep. I didn't want to go, but my job was important to me. Besides, once the meeting was over, I would have the rest of the day to do nothing but be with him. It sounded like the perfect way to spend a day.

"Where is that damn shoe?" I whispered, one flat in my hand and the other nowhere to be seen. I looked under the bed, under Aiden's clothes, on the porch, even in the gigantic closet attached to the huge bedroom.

As I searched and kept discovering more rooms, I wondered just what kind of assistant Aiden was. His room was nicer than Kathryn's. I paused for a moment as it hit me.

This had to be his boss's room and he had brought me here to impress me. I hoped Ben didn't mind and was out enjoying himself somewhere. We were definitely staying in my room after this, though. I didn't want to be doing the naked dance in someone else's room.

"Fine, you stupid shoe. Stay here," I whispered into empty air. I could not for the life of me find it. I blew out a breath of frustration, making a strand of hair flutter up from my face. I liked these shoes, but I would just have to find them later. Aiden could help me look. The *later* part of that thought made me smile. There was going to be a later.

I took one last peek at Aiden's sleeping form, giggling at how he had turned himself into a burrito, and carefully escaped. The world outside still smelled of rain. I took a deep breath, enjoying the way the salty air of the ocean mixed with the clean scent of freshly watered tropical plants. I filed the fragrance away in my memory as something wonderful.

"Good morning," a familiar voice interrupted my thoughts. Walking up the path was Kathryn in exercise clothes heading to the gym for a quick workout before the meeting. I wondered just how walk-of-shame-y I looked wearing a wet dress and missing my left shoe.

"Good morning," I replied cheerfully. I pulled away from Aiden's door and began to hurry back toward my own.

"Did you just come out of Mr. Hayes' suite?" She looked pointedly at my wet dress and I blushed hot enough steam should have come off the fabric.

"Mr. Hayes? No, no." I shook my head. At least I wasn't sleeping with the billionaire. I'm sure that was a conflict of interest somewhere. "That's where his assistant, Aiden, is staying today."

Kathryn frowned. "Mr. Hayes doesn't have an assistant. He has a bodyguard named Ben, but no assistant. Especially not one with the same name."

"You must be mistaken," I stammered. "Mr. Hayes is in his sixties and the man in there is barely thirty. There's no way that's Mr. Hayes."

She chuckled and shook her head. "You're thinking of Gerald Hayes. He founded the company, but his sons, Aiden and Logan run the company. Aiden Hayes is the Travel, Inc. representative that is scheduled to be here."

"Oh..." I swallowed hard and felt like my knees were going to give out. "Oh, boy."

Kathryn cocked her head to the side, apparently amused at my surprise. To be honest, thinking a billionaire was an assistant would be hilarious. I would be amused too if it hadn't been me. "Did you really think *Aiden Hayes* was an assistant?"

I nodded. "I did. The file you gave me was on Gerald Hayes and barely mentioned his sons. I should have put the names together, but..." I put my hands over my face as I realized just who I had been sleeping with. A billionaire. An honest to God billionaire. "I am such an idiot."

Kathryn pulled my hands from my face. "Not an idiot. Just blind is all."

A billionaire. Aiden was a freaking billionaire. And I had just spent the past few days treating him like a colleague instead of a boss. Teasing him. His pinky toe was worth more than my annual salary. My new really good salary. No wonder he hadn't worried about how much the dinner had cost last night. It could have cost a small house and he wouldn't have even seen a dip in his bank account.

She must have seen the horror swirling around in my eyes as I realized that I was way out of my depth. I was meant to date men who worked as copy-editors or were in school for something, not billionaires. Billionaires were supposed to date actresses or models. Not me.

"Lena." Kathryn used her lawyer voice to focus me. "Lena, you're okay. It doesn't matter that he's a billionaire. He's just a person and you haven't done anything wrong."

"What am I doing?" I whispered, more for me than for her. I knew I was in shock and this wouldn't matter near as much in a few minutes, but I let myself have a freak-out moment. I had just found out he wasn't at all what I thought. "How did I fall for a billionaire?"

"*You fell for a billionaire?* For Aiden Hayes?" Kathryn repeated it like I had just admitted I was guilty of murder. She tightened her grip on my hands to get my attention. "You need to be careful not to get attached to him, Lena. He isn't exactly known for his loyalty to his girlfriends. You're too good for the likes of him."

"What?" I tried to shake my hands free, but Kathryn held tight. Her lips pressed to a thin line. "He wouldn't do that..."

Kathryn evaluated my face and sighed at what she found there. "Just, take your time with him. I suppose it's good that you thought he was an assistant. At least you know your feelings for him are genuine and not bought. Just be careful. The last girl in your position with Aiden didn't fare well when he left her."

"What do you mean?"

"He dated a secretary a while back. Not his own- not even in the same company, but still a secretary. When his father found out it was getting serious, he had her fired. She had to move to a new state because no one would hire her after that." Kathryn glanced from side to side, making sure we were alone. "Gerald Hayes wants the best for his eldest. Flings he will tolerate, but the woman who will bear his grandchild... it's incredibly hypocritical given his own past, but that's what it is."

I tried my best to absorb that blow without it knocking me off my feet. "So, it's not Aiden, so much as his father that I should be afraid of?"

Kathryn sighed. "Yes and no. Aiden didn't stand up for the girl. He let her go. I heard he got her a better job elsewhere, but my point is that he didn't fight for her."

*Would he fight for me?* When he found out I wasn't what I had claimed to be, I knew he wouldn't. Yet, that didn't diminish what I felt for him. How much I ached for his body and just wanted to talk to him for hours.

My hands fell to my sides when Kathryn released them. Without Kathryn as my anchor, my world was spinning out of control with new information. I just wanted to go take a shower and sit by myself to think things out for a bit. I just needed to think.

"Make sure if you pursue him when we are no longer in the safety of the Caribbean that he will fight for you." Kathryn stepped back, opening up the path for me. "I can only protect you so much. Gerald Hayes has more influence than I do."

I nodded slowly. "I understand. Thank you, Kathryn."

Kathryn leaned forward as if she were going to hug me, but stopped short. She was a lawyer and being touchy wasn't her strong suit. I had never seen her give anyone more than a polite handshake. She skipped the hug and just patted my shoulder instead. "Of course," she said and then quickly turned and headed for the gym.

I walked to my room in a daze. The door beeped open and cold air rushed out into the tropical morning as I arrived. I stood in the doorway, letting the air escape. I didn't move until the air conditioner kicked on and surprised me with the new noise. Stepping inside, I closed the door and leaned against it, listening to the electrical whine of the motor cool the room. My mind bounced from thought to thought, but kept coming to settle back on one.

Aiden was a billionaire.

## CHAPTER 18

*I* sat outside on the resort's restaurant patio, staring at the melting ice at the bottom of my cup. Lunch had been hours ago, but I hadn't moved yet and had no intention of doing so. My plate was only half eaten, but as long as I pretended to keep munching, the busboy left me alone. It was quiet here with the other diners all off exploring the resort. I needed to think.

Kathryn's big meeting had gone well, and despite my brain being elsewhere I had managed to take decent notes for her. I couldn't say exactly what the meeting had even been about, but I had three typed pages of information. I'd figure it out when I typed up the minutes later.

Instead of paying attention to if the current measures to prevent litigation were working, I had been thinking of Aiden and the fact that he was a billionaire and what that meant for us as a couple.

All the signs that he was more than just an assistant had been there, but I had just been too enamored to see them. His clothes and shoes were nicer than even the things Kathryn had bought me for work, but I had just thought he had worked at his job longer and had earned better clothes. I had excused his renting a boat and the ability to drive it as quirks. Even his super swanky suite I had let myself believe was his boss's. All the facts had been there. I had just been blind and stupid.

He never said he was an assistant. I had assumed that. Granted, he hadn't done anything to change that opinion by telling me all the expensive activities were comped. I shook my head, feeling like an idiot. I had told him the romantic dinner on the beach had been too much. That had been pocket change.

A billionaire. I couldn't get my head around it. That much money just didn't seem even possible to me. He never had to worry about rent or the price of gas, or even if he had to pick between the sale toilet paper and the brand name. Hell, he probably had chinchilla fur toilet paper. I was having trouble just trying to imagine what kind of opulence he must be used to. He was so far out of my league, we weren't even playing the same sport anymore.

If he had chinchilla fur toilet paper, what did he see in me? No wonder he wanted me to be a lawyer. A lawyer could understand his world. What hope did a nearly broke paralegal have of understanding the life of a billionaire? It was like a fish trying to understand the life of a bird.

I shook the ice in my cup. It would be completely melted soon. Did his money change the way I felt about him? That was an easy question to answer. No, it didn't. I had fallen for him long before I knew he had money. Just thinking of those hazel eyes and the way his whole face lit up when he smiled, I knew I loved him. I had thought he walked on water back when I was sure we were in the same tax bracket.

My eyes widened as I realized what I just admitted to myself. I loved him. I had loved him from the minute he had taken my books and walked me upstairs. It didn't matter to me if he was a billionaire or a hundredaire.

My hand shook as I set the cup down. *I loved him.* I had never been in love like this before and that scared me more than his money. I felt so deeply for him that it made my whole body ache. The fact that he had a history of abandoning women like me was terrifying. If he left me, I would shatter. I needed him in my life like I needed the sun.

But he was a billionaire and I was close to broke. He probably spent more money on that chinchilla fur toilet paper than I made in a year. He deserved someone better than a girl just struggling to make rent and working like crazy for a scholarship. It didn't matter to me what the size of his bank account was, but I wondered if the size of mine mattered to him.

"Is this seat taken?" Aiden's voice cut through my thoughts like a hot knife through butter. I looked up to see him haloed in the sunlight.

"As long as the guy I'm dating doesn't see you," I replied. I couldn't help but smile when I saw him. With him in front of me, I could almost forget what he was. "But you look stronger than him, so you can probably take him in a fight."

"It's just because I ate my Wheaties this morning," he explained taking the seat across from me. Sunlight still highlighted his hair, turning it to honey gold. "How'd your meeting go?"

"Fine." I chewed on my lower lip. I needed to confess to him and get the billionaire issue out in the open. It was the only way I was going to stay sane for the next three days on the island with him. "I ran into Kathryn when I came out of your room this morning."

"Okay..." He shrugged like running into my boss was nothing and popped one of the fries from my plate into his mouth. His nose wrinkled up in disgust at the cold, soggy fry. "How long have you been sitting here?"

"She informed me that I had just come out of Mr. Hayes' room. The Mr. Hayes that run Travel, Inc. and is worth billions." I picked at the cuticle on my thumb, nervous at what was going to happen next. "It kind of gave me a surprise this morning."

Aiden put down the second french fry that was on its way to his mouth . "And?"

"I thought you were an assistant," I admitted, feeling exponentially more stupid with every word that left my mouth. "I thought Ben the bodyguard was your boss."

Aiden's eyes focused completely on me as he settled into his chair. "I wasn't completely sure you didn't know until this moment, but I suspected." He paused and then smiled. "It was actually refreshingly wonderful that you didn't know."

"Wonderful? How could not knowing who you are be wonderful? I didn't know the one thing that everyone else knows does." I looked up at him, feeling lost. Everyone else on this island knew who Aiden was and gave him the respect he deserved. I told him that he spent too much on dinner.

"It's the one thing I wish people didn't know," Aiden explained softly. "People see me and think that I'm a walking ATM. It's worse than just being wealthy, because every single person knows I can afford anything, so they don't even bother pretending to be polite about it. Do you know how many people tell me not to spend my money on them? One."

"Who?" I asked, already knowing the answer.

The corners of Aiden's eyes crinkled with warmth as he smiled. "You." He reached across the table for my hands. It felt good to be touched by him. "You are the best thing that's happened to me in a long time."

"So, you're actually okay with having a dumb girlfriend that doesn't recognize the signs of a man with money?" I asked. I still felt stupid for being so oblivious.

"You are not dumb," he assured me. "And I'm very okay with it. Are you okay dating a billionaire?"

"Honestly, I'm still processing it." I looked up to see his smile falter and my heart dropped. "I thought you were a normal guy and I just found out that you make my year's salary in an hour. It's just kind of a rough transition. I'm having to change my expectations a little."

His brow tightened. "What do you mean?"

"I was imagining you picking me up in a five year old car with a banged up headlight, and now I'm trying to imagine a helicopter. I was thinking that date night would be dinner at a drive-thru and then cramming into a crowded movie theater instead of five-star dining and opera." I looked up at him and shrugged. I felt incredibly overwhelmed by his wealth. "I don't even know how to ride in a limo, let alone a helicopter."

He squeezed my hands and smiled. "Limos are just like cars, only bigger."

"It's just..." Here was the hard part. Here was where I had to tell him that I didn't fit in his world. I couldn't look at him. "I don't know how to handle helicopters and opera. I don't know if I'm good enough for you."

He didn't immediately say anything and I could feel the silence like a weight. I had just given him an out and now I had to wait for him to take it. I didn't want him to, but I needed to give him the chance.

He let go of my hands and stood. My stomach tightened

into a cold ball. He was going to leave and he had every right to. I wasn't worthy of a billionaire.

Instead of leaving, though, he came and knelt by my chair. I stared at the ground, heart pounding and head unsure. He dipped his beautiful head until he was in my line of sight and I had to look at him. He was smiling.

"You are more than good enough for me," he said softly. He touched my cheek so tenderly my heart was ready to explode. "If anything, you're too good."

I let out a nervous breath that sounded almost like a giggle. "You're okay with dating a girl with about three hundred dollars in her bank account? It's going to make it a little tough for me to split the bill at the opera."

He grinned. "The guy's supposed to pay anyway on a date."

I wasn't sure if he kissed me, or if I kissed him. Either way, our lips connected just the way they were supposed to. It was the sweetest kiss I had ever had. It was love.

He returned to his chair, grinning at me as he picked up the cold french fry again. "You know, I can get you fresh ones," I offered as he made a face as the second fry was no better than the first.

"Where's the fun in that?" he asked with a laugh and picked up another. I shook my head at him. He held up the fry in midair, a question crossing his brow. "You only have three hundred dollars? I thought lawyers made more than that."

I stared at him for a moment, trying to figure out how to say this. I needed to tell him that I wasn't the lawyer he thought I was. This was my chance to make sure all our secrets were cleared out before they came between us and ruined things.

"I'm sorry," Aiden apologized, mortification filling his

face. "That was incredibly rude of me to ask you about your money. You don't have to answer that."

"No, it's actually something I need to tell you." I swallowed down the fear. He would understand. He just said that he cared for me. I loved him for him and not his bank account. He loved me and not the fact that I was a lawyer. I could do this. I took a deep breath.

"There you are!" Kathryn exclaimed, interrupting the pulsating silence between us. Her normally calm demeanor was gone and she looked about ready to melt into pure panic at any moment. "I've been looking everywhere for you! The plane's being prepped right now. We have to go."

"Plane?" I repeated, confused. "What plane?"

"Smith had a heart attack last night," Kathryn explained as she grabbed my hand to pull me up from my chair. "I just found out after the meeting because for some god-forsaken reason, the second chair thought he could handle it and didn't call in Ward or let the judge know right away."

"Holy shit," I gasped. This was bad. Super bad.

"It just gets worse from there. The news is calling it the 'Dallas Disaster.'" Kathryn let go of my hand once I was standing. "It's an all-hands-on-deck emergency. I had someone pack your bags and they're already on the plane. We have to leave right now."

I looked over at Aiden. I couldn't leave things like this. I had to tell him the truth. I was so close. "But..."

"Go. They need you. You can tell me whatever it was later." His face was pure understanding. He was a wonderful man, no matter what had happened between him and that secretary.

"I'll be right behind you," I promised Kathryn. She pursed her lips unhappily, but nodded. She started walking and I knew I only had a second or two to catch up.

I knelt by Aiden's chair, searching for the magic words that would tell him everything I needed him to know. I didn't have time. Instead, I put my hands on either side of his face and kissed him. He leaned into me, taking everything I had to give. I put all my emotions, all the things I wanted to say and couldn't find the words or the time to tell him into my kiss, hoping he would understand.

"I love you," I whispered as my lips left his. He tensed slightly under my fingertips, but I didn't stop my words. "I love you not because you're a billionaire, but because you're Aiden. I love who you are, not what you are."

I didn't stop to see his reaction. I just turned and ran before he could answer and break my heart. I didn't stop running until I caught up to Kathryn. She was already in a taxi and on her phone. I was breathing hard as I hopped inside. The car door had barely shut when the cab driver hit the gas.

I looked back at the way I had just come. No one was there. I had this romantic notion in my head that he would be there. That he would follow me when I told him I loved him. I didn't want him to push me away, and I suddenly regretted saying the words that were best guaranteed to do so. I closed my eyes to keep the tears inside as I tried not to think of what his absence meant.

## CHAPTER 19

*I* buckled my seat on the private jet and stared numbly out the window. I knew he wouldn't come, but I kept hoping Aiden would show up out on the runway to show me he cared. I kept staring down the long runway, searching for his face as he came to tell me he loved me too.

Kathryn finished her phone call and went straight into the next, only pausing to transition to the jet's phone instead of her cell. I knew I would have a few more minutes to myself before she would be ready to give me a list of things to do.

My laptop was already charging in a little docking station next to my seat. I opened it, found the jet's wifi. I had stayed on top of my work emails using the resort's internet connection, but I had specifically avoided using my computer for anything but work.

I pulled up a search page and paused, my fingers hovering over the keys.

All I had to do was type in Aiden's name and I would

know everything about him. I would have pictures and newspaper articles and everything the cyber-stalker in me could want. I would know all the secrets he had told me the night before, but this time they would be printed in black and white.

I typed his name and hit enter before I could stop myself.

Search results filed in and the pit of my stomach dropped.

I had been expecting news articles on Travel, Inc., business reports, perhaps some charity work, and even some photographs from galas and events. Instead, almost every entry was for his latest flavor of the week model or actress.

Page after page of photos of him with various beauties. Stunning, long-legged girls that made me look like a chubby freak. Three girls getting out of his limo with their hair mussed . Twins sitting with him at his center court seats. Aiden front and center at a premier lingerie show. His smiling face looked up at me from the computer screen. They all hung off of his arms like decorative jewelry, but never the same girl twice.

I found an article about the secretary and clicked on the link, unsure of what I hoped to find.

*...Aiden is a great guy," Stephani Zaptos said in one of her rare interviews. "I just didn't fit into his world. It really worked out for the best and I'm appreciative of everything he's done for me."*

*Inside sources theorize Stephani was paid off by Aiden Hayes' overprotective father, Gerald Hayes to keep her from gold-digging. As Hayes Sr. has several embarrassing and expensive sexual*

*liaisons recently come to light, it would only make sense that he would try and protect his sons' from the same thing.*

*There is also speculation that Hayes Sr. may have blackballed the secretary in retaliation for Aiden and his brother edging their father out of the company. Sources close to the Hayes state that Gerald is not appreciative of his forced retirement by his sons.*

*Others simply suggest that Zaptos was simply just another one of Aiden's flavor of the week liaisons. All we here at Tabloid 34 know is that Aiden Hayes, billionaire playboy, is back on the market.*

I STARED AT THE PICTURES, barely recognizing the man in them. They all looked like the Aiden I had fallen in love with, but I couldn't believe them. I couldn't believe *him*. The more I looked at the pictures, the more I realized I had no idea who Aiden really was.

Three days was not enough to know someone, and certainly not enough to fall in love. The realization hit me hard enough to make me gasp.

*Told you so*, my brain told my heart. I didn't want to believe it, but the proof that I didn't actually know Aiden was staring me in the face. He was too perfect to have been real. He had played me.

*"I could be a very different person than the one you think you know. How do you know that I'm not a terrible person?"* Aiden's words echoed in my head.

He was right. I didn't know him. I didn't know him at all, yet I had just told him that I loved him.

No wonder he hadn't come after me.

Even as I looked at the pictures of him with other women, I wanted to excuse him. I wanted the man I met on the island to be the real one. We had been so happy. He had invited me to his brother's wedding. But, it had all been a lie.

I scrubbed my face with my hands. I couldn't believe I was such a gullible idiot. I didn't deserve to get into Harvard. I didn't deserve to get into a community college intro to law course. Aiden Hayes had duped me completely and in more ways than one.

I slammed my laptop shut, wanting to make the images disappear from my mind just as easily. I didn't know him. I needed to forget about him like he was going to forget about me. I didn't look like the supermodels in those pictures, and there was no logical explanation why he would ever chose me over one of them. He didn't love me. He never had.

I was a fling. A way to stay entertained during a business meeting.

Kathryn hung up the phone and let out a huge sigh of frustration. "Sorry to interrupt your lunch with Mr. Hayes," she apologized, leaning back in her seat and rubbing her temples.

"Don't worry about it," I mumbled, putting my laptop back in its station and staring out the window.

Kathryn frowned and stopped rubbing her head to look at me. "You okay?"

I shook my head no, knowing that despite my best efforts to keep my emotions locked up, they have to be written across my face. I knew if I said his name, I'd lose it and I wasn't ready to cry in front of Kathryn. I wasn't ready to cry at all.

"No, but I don't want to talk about it." I took a shaky breath and wiped my hands across my cheeks to catch any tears that might have escaped. "Tell me more about the Dallas Disaster. Where are we going now and what do you need me to do?"

Kathryn evaluated me for a moment, and then nodded slowly. "Okay." She leaned back into her chair again as the engine started to rumble. "We are flying aback to Chicago to do damage control."

"What about Smith?" I asked, sitting up straight. "You said he had a heart attack-- is he...?"

"Elijah's going to be fine. He just got out of surgery. He had a double bypass and is expected to make a full recovery." She smiled at the good news and then sighed. "But there's no way he's going to be able to do this case."

"I'm glad he's okay." Even though the man had given my spot at the trial to Alexa, I wanted him to be all right. He was still an amazing lawyer. "Who will be taking over for him?"

"Derek Johnson. He's just getting to Houston now." Kathryn raised her voice to be heard over the whine of the engines as they powered up for takeoff.

"Why wasn't Derek second chair in the first place? He's the one Smith's been grooming to take over all his criminal defense cases when he retires anyway." It felt good to focus my brain on something other than Aiden. Work was something I understood.

"He was. His flight in last night was delayed." Kathryn ran her fingers through her hair and looked up at the ceiling as the plane fought gravity. "It's chaos and I'm still sorting out the details."

"You said the judge wasn't informed. Who was second chair until Derek arrived and why didn't they call anybody?" I asked. I couldn't think of anyone that stupid at our firm.

"Calvin was second chair," Kathryn answered. I guess I did know someone that stupid. "What I'm hearing is that Calvin waited to inform everyone because he tried to convince the client to let him make the opening statements."

"What!?" I nearly fell out of my seat in surprise, even with the seat belt on.

"Luckily, the client has watched an episode of "Law and Order" in his lifetime and realized that was a bad idea." Kathryn sounded completely exasperated. She closed her eyes and pinched the bridge of her nose like she was getting a headache. Given the mess that was going on with her firm, I would have been surprised if she didn't have one. "He refused, figuring that his lawyer having a heart attack was a good reason to delay a trial. This whole thing could have been much, much worse. But, the paperwork and publicity surrounding this thing is still a nightmare."

"Calvin's not a bad lawyer, but I can't believe he would do something like that," I said shaking my head in disbelief.

"He saw an opportunity to be in the limelight," Kathryn explained with a shrug. "It's not often a low-level lawyer is presented with an opportunity to be on center stage. If he had pulled it off, he would have been offered partner at a dozen firms. Opportunity does things to people."

"More likely Alexa saw the opportunity." I almost felt sorry for Calvin. "Is he going to be fired?"

"Probably. We have to make sure that's what actually happened, and we can't do that until Smith wakes up from his surgery." She shrugged without pity. Calvin had put the reputation of her firm on the line.

"Wow," I mouthed. This was a disaster. "What do you need me to do?"

Kathryn didn't open her eyes. "You're going to need a pen."

I was in for a lot of work. *But, at least it will keep your mind off Aiden*, I told myself. Except, I knew there was nothing short of a coma that would keep me from thinking of him.

## CHAPTER 20

"Did you get ahold of the reporter for the Houston Daily?" Kathryn asked.

"Yes, ma'am. I scheduled the official interview with Derek's secretary and had the reporter send his questions to her ahead of time," I answered checking off another item on my list. If I didn't have a calendar in front of me I wouldn't have known what day it was we were so busy. I hadn't been home since the flight back, yet I remembered falling asleep on one of the couches in Kathryn's office at least twice.

"Good. What about the files for tomorrow-"

"I got those done too. They've been faxed and I checked with the courthouse that they were received," I answered quickly. "Now, you need to get going. You have a meeting with the Mayor and if you are late or reschedule your secretary will skin me alive. She said I would have to handle all the phone calls from him and you don't pay me enough for that."

I got up from my desk and handed her the suit jacket hanging on the wall behind me. I could tell she was still in emergency mode and was having a hard time leaving the office for anything short of a five-alarm fire. Considering we both were still wearing the same clothes from two days ago, I wasn't much better.

"Kathryn," I said gently as I put the jacket in her hands. "I've got things under control for at least three hours. Derek has been in constant communication and Mr. Smith is practically trying to run the trial from his hospital bed. You can go to your lunch meeting. Besides, he's is going to be here any minute."

She frowned. "But the-"

"No butts," I told her firmly. "Lunch."

Kathryn smiled as she shrugged into her jacket. "When'd you learn to be bossy? I thought I hired a mouse."

"It's all the coffee," I replied with a shrug as sat back at my desk to continue on my lists. The coffee was good, but it wasn't what was powering me through the days.

"Then remind me to get you more for Christmas," she murmured as she pulled her hair out from under the stylish jacket. "I'll have my phone on the whole time. Call me immediately if anything changes."

"Scout's honor," I promised, holding up three fingers. "Have a good time."

"It's just quick follow up with Gerald Hayes in my office before lunch." Kathryn paused before leaving. "Lena?"

"Yeah?" I looked up, ready to add whatever she needed to my to-do list.

"I don't know what happened to you on that island, but whatever it was, you needed it." She smiled, warming her features. "You did excellent work before we left, but you didn't take charge. Since we've been back, you've been a one-woman show. If it's the coffee giving you this spark, I'll buy you a year's supply."

I beamed at the compliment. "I like the hazelnut flavor

in the blue cups and I'm pretty sure the creamer in the fridge has something to do with it too."

"You got it." Kathryn laughed. She paused at my desk. "Before I go, I wanted you to know I sent in my letter of recommendation for you to Harvard."

"Thank you. I appreciate it."

"If they don't let you in, they're going to have a very unhappy supporting alumni." She winked. "Though, I wouldn't mind if it means getting to keep you around the office a little while longer."

"I really appreciate that, but you need to get in your office or he'll be there before you," I warned her with a smile. "Don't make me call security on you."

"There's that confidence again." Kathryn glared good-naturedly at me. "Hazelnut in the blue cups it is."

I looked up in time to see her swish into her office and start picking things up. I was doing my best to ignore the fact that she was having a meeting with Aiden's father. I kept telling myself that Gerald Hayes and Aiden Hayes were two entirely separate people and that arrival of one did not mean the other would show as well.

My coffee mug was only half empty, but I still had a lot of work to do and a full cup sounded like a good way to start. Before I left my desk though, I checked my phone and my email, just in case something new had come in.

There were a couple new interoffice notices, but nothing I wanted to see. Nothing from Aiden. It had been almost three days since our hasty departure and my heartfelt admission of love, but I hadn't heard a word from him.

The silence was what was fueling me, not the coffee.

I stood up and rolled my shoulders. I had been staring at my computer screen and on the phone all day and now I had nasty crick in my neck. I checked my inbox one last time before picking up my mug. Nothing.

I dumped my mug out into the sink and set it on the silver tray of the K-cup coffee machine before opening the cabinet to look at the coffee selection. The hazelnut flavored blue cups were gone, so I settled for a green morning blend instead. *No,* I thought to myself, *it definitely wasn't the coffee.*

I raised the silver handle to place the coffee pod in the machine. The coffee maker was certainly getting a workout this week. The entire office was staying late trying to catch up on the Dallas Disaster in addition to their regular workloads. Coffee pods were becoming rare commodities. There was a used K-cup inside, and so I reached in and grabbed it. The empty cup was still hot from the last user and it burned my fingers. I hissed, more from surprise than pain, and flung it into the trash.

Two and a half days. I had held out hope that there would be a message waiting for me when I stepped off the plane. I was sure there would be a phone call that evening. I had been positive that he would at least leave me a note on my desk the next day. But nothing came. A full day of nothing, followed by another. And still nothing today. It was time to accept that he was never going to say anything.

I sucked on my offended fingers as I finished making my coffee. I should have known that he wasn't going to follow me. I had told him I loved him after just three days. Any sane man would avoid a woman like that. Especially one with a playboy history like Aiden. I had been a fling. Something fun to pass the time at a boring convention.

It hurt, and not just my fingers. I couldn't help that I still loved him. I thought knowing the truth about him would change my feelings, but it didn't. The pictures on the internet were just pictures. I loved the man who brought me dinner, took me fishing, and got caught in the rain with me.

I knew he must not feel the same. Two days of silence suggested otherwise. I had just been his latest flavor of the week. I had thought I was different. I had thought we had something special, but every hour that went by without a word just told me otherwise.

And so, I buried myself in work. If I kept busy, I didn't think quite so much about him or what I had said. Looking through witness statements and working on logistics kept me from remembering the smell of his hair and the way his eyes sparkled when he smiled. Quarterly reports banished the way his laughter made me smile. It was a blatant lie I told myself to make me feel better, but it was what got me through the day.

I had the choice to sit and mope, or to let the experience make me stronger. For once in my life, I chose stronger. I was going to use this as the opportunity to become the person I wanted to be. The person Aiden showed me I could be.

I was working hard on not letting anyone walk over me again. Not even Alexa. When I first met Aiden, I had believed I was worthwhile simply because he did. Now, I realized that even though he wasn't here or even still believed it himself, I did. I was worthwhile because I believed in me. If Aiden did nothing else for me, he at least gave me the chance to believe in myself. He had changed me and I was going to make sure it was for the better.

The coffee finished and my stomach grumbled. Kathryn had arranged for meals since we were all working late this week, but it wasn't time for lunch to arrive yet. I remembered seeing a pizza guy walk into the conference room late last night. If I was lucky, there still might be a couple of slices left. I set my coffee on my desk so I wouldn't have to juggle it and a plate, and went on the hunt for leftovers.

The conference room was a bust. All that was left of the pizza was empty boxes and bare plates. I sighed and headed for the library. Darcie usually had some cookies stashed in her desk. If I asked nicely and told her it would make me feel better about Aiden, she would happily give the me a couple to dip in my coffee while I worked.

"Lena," Kathryn's voice called to me. I turned to see her standing with an older, sadder version of Aiden. Looking at him made my heart twist. He was so very much like the man I loved, and yet so very different.

"What can I do for you, Ms. McDonald?" I asked, putting on my best professional smile.

"Mr. Hayes was interested in getting a copy of all the meeting minutes as well as the updated litigation forms," Kathryn explained. "Would you make sure they're on my desk by the time I return from lunch?"

"Of course." I looked to Mr. Hayes and saw brown eyes where his son had beautiful hazel. "Do you need anything else?"

"You must be the woman Aiden spoke of from the conference," Mr. Hayes said, evaluating me.. His voice was deeper and smokier than Aiden's.

I swallowed hard. "There were quite a few women at the conference," I replied, dodging his eyes.

While I doubted Aiden could have meant anyone else, this wasn't exactly a topic I was ready to discuss in the middle of the hallway, especially considering I had no idea what Aiden would have told his father about me.

"We really should be getting to lunch," Kathryn announced, stopping that path of questioning. "Thank you for those forms, Lena."

Mr. Hayes gave me one last look turning to leave with Kathryn. He and his son had the same shoulders and walked with the same confident stride. Empty loss caught in my throat.

"There she is." Alexa's voice cut through my hunger and heartsickness like a knife. If it had any more disdain, it would have melted through the floor. "There's Lena the *paralegal*."

I had barely seen a perfectly curled eyelash of Alexa since arriving. One of the first things Kathryn had done upon arriving back was to send out a new team of lawyers to Houston. Alexa and the rest of the lawyers from the Houston group had been sent back to Chicago with their tails between their legs. Alexa had the good sense to stay down in the Dungeons and away from Kathryn's domain, which meant she had stayed away from me as well.

But now, she was standing in the middle of the hallway with Aiden.

Announcing my job title.

Now he knew.

My chest tightened and my stomach started flip-flopped so hard I was certain I'd never want to eat again. My forehead and stomach flushed with heat while my hands and shoulders turned to ice. He was here. Over two days of silence and now he was here, standing in my office building next to the woman who wanted to ruin my life.

He looked so handsome and fit the part of the billionaire perfectly today. There was no way anyone could mistake him for an assistant. He wore a strong black suit that fit him like the designer had made the suit with him in it. Silver cufflinks matched his tie and the ascot folded elegantly in his left breast pocket. I didn't know that a man could look that good in a suit without Photoshop.

His hair was neatly combed back and picture perfect. Not a honey curl out of place. He had shaved recently, so his jaw was smooth and clean under dark, unreadable eyes. It was the eyes that made my heart quiver. They were focused entirely on me.

"Imagine my surprise to find a billionaire in my office," Alexa told the crowd starting to gather in the hallway. Gerald Hayes stopped in his tracks and turned to see what was going on, with Kathryn right next to him. He looked shocked. Alexa smiled at me like a snake. "He seemed to think it was yours, Lena. I informed him that paralegals don't have offices like lawyers do."

I didn't move. She was baiting me and I wasn't going to take it. Besides, my body didn't seem to be working. I couldn't move and I certainly couldn't think of anything to say. All I could do was stare at Aiden. This was not the way I wanted him to find out I wasn't a lawyer, and this was most certainly not the way I wanted his father to find out who I was.

Alexa put her hand on Aiden's coat lapel. I knew they had met once at a legal function, but it still felt incredibly forward. She looked stunning in her pencil skirt and silk blouse draped up against him. Like something that belonged on a movie poster. "Whatever you need Lena for," she purred to Aiden. "I'm sure I can do it better. She's barely more than a poorly trained secretary."

There was no doubt exactly what she meant. Something inside of me broke free. Something that fed on hazelnut coffee from the blue cups.

"Shut up, Alexa."

Alexa's hand didn't drop from Aiden's lapel, but she did startle. "What did you say to me?"

"I said shut up." My tongue felt thick, but I wasn't about

to stop. She was touching the man I loved. Even if he didn't want me anymore, there was no way in hell I was going to let her anywhere near him. I took a confident step forward, my head held high.

"I have an office, Alexa and it's actually bigger than yours." Her dark eyes met mine and for the first time I saw why she hated me so much. She was afraid of me.

Alexa sneered. "You think you're so special--

Kathryn stepped forward and cut her off. "Alright, Alexa. I've had about enough of this. You are embarrassing us in front of a client."

Alexa turned as if she was going to bite the head off of the person talking to her. When she saw it was Kathryn, her eyes lowered.

"Your team was responsible for this disaster, and we've had to work around the clock to fix *your* mistake. You've done nothing but create extra work for Lena, and I'm tired of it. You've never done a damn thing around here, and nobody's going to notice when you get fired at the end of the week anyway."

Alexa lifted her eyes. "Ms. McDonald, I-"

Kathryn laughed an obviously fake laugh. "This debacle has given this firm so much bad press, you'll be lucky to ever get even a paralegal job again."

My jaw should have dropped at the way Alexa was being treated, but I knew she had it coming. Karma had a way of coming for us all.

I stepped forward, and with a new self confidence. "Looks like you're not better than me after all." I took another step forward. "So get your hands off him."

Alexa's hand dropped instinctively to the authority in my voice. Her eyes darted to the observing crowd and she paled. There wasn't a sympathetic face among them.

"You have no idea the mistake you just made," she hissed.

I smiled slowly. She had nothing and we both knew it. For the first time ever, I wasn't afraid of her. I had found my inner strength, and no one, not Alexa and not even Aiden was going to take it away from me.

My smile made her pale more than looking at the crowd had. She had no power over me anymore and now she knew it. I didn't even bother watch as wiggled her way back downstairs through the crowd.

I took a deep breath. It came in shaky and wasn't at all calming. Just because I had inner strength didn't mean my heart couldn't be broken.

"Hello, Mr. Hayes," I said politely, turning slightly to face him directly. My voice shook at his name. "I wasn't expecting you. Please, let me show you to my office."

I didn't wait to hear his answer as I spun and started walking back toward my desk. Kathryn could handle the other Mr. Hayes and the crowd on her own.

From the corner of my eye I could see Darcie giving me a huge thumb's up from the library. I had told her everything about my trip. Her confidence in me made it easier to believe that I could do this. I grinned nervously at her and kept walking.

I could hear him behind me as well as the murmurs of people returning to their offices. Alexa liked a crowd, but I didn't. I could feel everyone's eyes on me as I held open the door to the small space I called my own. As he passed I could smell his shampoo and it made me go weak in the knees with the memory of my hair tangled in his fingers.

I took another deep breath that still did nothing to calm my nerves, holding onto the door handle for an extra moment trying to steady myself before I had to turn around and face him. I had no idea what was going to happen next, but I closed the door anyway.

"Lena...." His voice was as soft as the hand he placed on my shoulder. I couldn't help but stiffen at his touch. It felt so wonderful, yet so far from what I could have. I couldn't turn from the door to look at him because I knew if I did, I would burst into tears.

He pulled gently. "Lena, look at me."

I took a deep breath in, hoping that eventually these breaths would become calming, and reluctantly turned to face him.

He was so damn handsome he took my breath away. Every inch of him was perfect. I wanted to reach out and touch him, to kiss him again, but was terrified at the same time. My new found courage had completely deserted me when faced with the thing I wanted and feared most. The last few days of being alone tugged at my mind, telling me I needed to run before he could hurt me again.

But my feet wouldn't move. Couldn't move. I didn't want to leave him. It broke my heart to be near him and know that it was all going to officially end. He was here to tell me that he didn't want a paralegal. He had wanted a lawyer and someone who didn't lie or not know about his money. He wanted someone befitting a billionaire.

He let go of my shoulder and put his finger and thumb to my chin. The movement was gentle, but he tipped my chin up so I would look at his face instead of staring at his tie. I didn't want to look into his eyes because I knew I would just fall in love with him all over again.

"You left this," he said, pulling something out from the inside pocket of his suit jacket. It was the shoe I had lost in his room on our last day. He held it out in front of him like a rope to a drowning man. I gasped, looking up into his hazel eyes. Suddenly, I wasn't sure which one of us needed the lifeline more.

I raised my hand out to touch the shoe, but didn't take it. I wasn't sure if I could. I needed to know if this was what I thought and hoped it was. I needed to know I would be enough for a billionaire.

"I'm not a lawyer," I whispered. There. I said it. I just hoped it wasn't too little to late.

"I know." Aiden's voice shook but the hand holding the shoe was steady.

"I'm sorry you had to find out from Alexa," I said softly, looking at the shoe. "I just didn't know how to tell you."

"I knew before she announced it to your office."

I looked up from the shoe into his face. "What?"

"I knew you weren't a lawyer the day you arrived on the island."

"How?" My heart was threatening to shatter into a million pieces and the only thing holding me together was the fact we were both holding my shoe.

"I wanted to know who the amazing woman from the MSW law firm was," he said with a gentle smile. "It didn't take much to find out."

"But..." He knew. He knew I lied that whole time. "You didn't say anything..."

"I didn't want to embarrass you." He stared at the shoe in our hands. "I should have let you say something. I know you did try to tell me."

I wondered if he could feel me shaking through the shoe. I felt like a leaf in a thunderstorm. "Why are you here?" I asked. Despite his gentle tone, it had been over two days. Two days where I wasn't sure what he felt or if he even wanted me.

"When you said you..." He stumbled on his words and

stared at the shoe, brow furrowed and dark. "When you said you loved me, I didn't know what to do. I was so sure it was a lie."

My eyes flashed up to his, anger threatening to spill out of my broken quivering heart. "It wasn't a lie!"

"All my life, people have lied to me to get what they want. Usually it's money or power." He met my gaze, his hazel eyes full of honesty and heartache. "You fell in love with me without knowing I had either. I was just Aiden to you, and I couldn't fathom how that was possible. How could you love someone like me without expecting something in return?"

"I just wanted you," I whispered. All the hurt and tears I had suppressed and worked through since getting on the plane to leave were threatening to overwhelm me.

"It took me a day and a half to realize that I am a complete and utter idiot." He paused, his eyes enveloping me in their warmth. "You loved me for something no one else has. You loved me with no thought of any gain for yourself."

A small, hopeful smile lit his eyes. I didn't dare breathe in case this was all a dream.

"Lena Masterson, I love you. Not because you're a lawyer, but because you bring out the best in me. I want you to be a part of my life," he confessed. Every inch of his face shone with the truth of his words. "You are amazing in your own right, and it doesn't matter if you have letters after your name or not. You're funny, and kind; and you make me ridiculously happy. I like the person I am when I'm with you. You complete me."

I sniffled, my heart expanding in my chest to envelope the whole room. He loved me and wanted me regardless of what anyone else thought. The hand not holding the shoe reached up and touched my face. I realized I was crying, but it was with tears of joy.

"I love you, Lena." Aiden cupped my face and made me look at him. I peered into his eyes and could see that every word was true.

"I love you, too, Aiden," I whispered. My heart was ready to burst with joy.

"You are my fate, Lena," he whispered, holding me close. "I'm sorry it took me so long to light my candle. Do you think you can help me keep it lit?"

"Yes." I took the shoe and kissed him, not wanting to be apart from him for a second longer.

He pressed his hands into my hair, drawing me into him. I kissed him like a drowning man searching for air. My hands wrapped around his neck and mussed his hair. I had missed him so badly the past couple of days that I never wanted to spend another moment apart from him.

I fought the need to breathe for as long as possible. He pressed his forehead into mine and I could feel all the pieces of my heart knitting back together. His arms were strong and safe, promising me a future of love and devotion.

This was everything I could have hoped for. I looked up into the green over brown depths that led straight into Aiden's soul. They were so beautiful, not just in their coloring, but in what they were full of. Love. More than anything, when I looked into Aiden's eyes, I saw how we were fated and chose to find one another.

I kissed him again, wanting only to feel his heart beat with mine.

He loved me and I him. Together we would keep one another's candles lit with love and barefoot kisses.

## EPILOGUE

*I* take a deep breath and slip into my shoes.

*They aren't the shoes that brides usually wear on their wedding. These shoes are just simple black flats with sand stuck in the cracks near the toes.*

*"You ready?" My sister Louisa asks, peeking out through the door.*

*"Ready as I'm ever going to be," I say. Now that I have the shoes on, my nerves are settling. I know he loves me because these shoes prove it.*

*My mother fusses one last time with my dress. It's satin and lace and possibly the most beautiful wedding dress I have ever seen. I'm sure all brides think that of their dresses, but for mine, I'm sure of it.*

*I hear the music start inside the church.*

*"I love you, sweetheart," Mom says, giving me a kiss on the cheek. There are tears of pride in her eyes. She wipes the lipstick from her kiss off my cheek.*

*"I love you too, Momma," I whisper. She presses her lips together as tight as she can to keep from crying as she hurries out to take her seat.*

"She's so beautiful," I hear her tell my dad. He's waiting just outside the door. Once Darcie and Louisa leave, it will be my turn.

"See you up there," Darcie says with a grin.

"Hey," Louisa whispers. She fixes my veil and smiles. "If this is what it got you, I'm glad you missed dinner last year. I've never seen you so happy."

I nearly cry. It was a year ago that Aiden bought me dinner after a terrible day and a missed date with my sister. I hug her close, glad to have someone as wonderful as her in my life.

She pulls back and wipes at her eyes. "Don't make me cry or Darcie's going to beat me up."

We both laugh because we know it's true.

I follow her out the door and Dad takes my arm.

"You sure you want to do this?" he asks, guiding me to the back of the church. "I'll go get the car right now if you say the word."

"I love him, Daddy. A lot."

"I know. I just have to ask." He smiles, but there are tears welling up in his eyes. "You will be my little princess, forever. You know that, right?"

I wrap my arms around him and hold him tight. I am glad I'm still his little girl, even though I'm standing in a church in a wedding dress.

The wedding march begins and my stomach flutters. It's time.

I hold my father's arm as he walks me down the aisle. I glance to the sides, seeing friends and family. To my right, I see Noah and Izzy, waving and smiling. On my left, my cousin Emma and her husband Jack watch with huge smiles. My other cousin, Kaylee and her husband are at the front of the church trying to reign in a very boisterous little flower girl while Aiden's brother, Logan, makes silly faces at the child.

They all fade away as soon as I see Aiden.

*I don't see the suit that I helped him pick out. I don't see the boutonniere that my mother insisted upon. I only see his smile and the love he has for me in his eyes.*

*I give my father one last hug and kiss. He shakes Aiden's hand before reluctantly letting me go.*

*I'm smiling so wide it hurts and I'm afraid my heart is going to burst out of my chest at any moment its beating so hard.*

*"Dearly Beloved," the minister begins. I know the words. These are the words that are going to bind Aiden and I together so that we will never have to be apart again. The promises that we make here today to one another will be what guides us for the rest of our journey together.*

*The ceremony is short and sweet. I honestly am too excited to remember much of it. I put the important parts, the things I want to tell my children about someday firmly in my mind.*

*The way the ring felt when Aiden slid it on my finger and promised to love me for all time.*

*How easy and right it was to give him his ring and promise to love him.*

*The way the candles flickered as we each picked up our own solitary wick and joined them together to light a new candle. A candle that would burn through the night and chase away the dark.*

*But mostly, I know I will remember the kiss. The cocky smile Aiden wears when the minister tells him he may kiss me. How he reaches for me, drawing us together like magnets. In that kiss, I know that we are meant to be together forever. That this is fate.*

*All too soon the ceremony is over. I hold Aiden's hand as the church goes wild. Darcie's husband holds their tiny son, but he just smiles instead of waking up to the noise. Kathryn and the other lawyers cheer so loud it hurts my ears. It's almost as if there is a competition between my old law firm and the law students from my school.*

*Aiden and I dance down the aisle. Everyone is cheering. My mother is crying and my father is stoic, but I can see tears in his eyes. Even Aiden's father looks pleased. Darcie flashes me a thumbs up and I laugh. We escape out the back door. Ben motions us to follow him, a smile plastered across his face. He guides us to a small room, and turns to guard the door.*

*Aiden and I giggle and sneak inside. This might be the only moment we get to ourselves for the rest of the night. We have a big party planned, and while I'm excited to celebrate, I'm eternally grateful to Ben for giving us this moment to ourselves.*

*"I love you," Aiden whispers, caressing my cheek with his hand. "More than anything."*

*I lean into his touch, reveling in the soft stroke of his skin. I stand up on my tip toes and kiss his smile. He laughs, wrapping me up in his arms and lifting me up in the air.*

*My shoes slide off my feet but I don't care. I'm kissing the man I love. The man who is not only my best friend, but now my husband.*

*He sets me down and I sneak in one last barefoot kiss before he helps me slide my shoes back on.*

*Then together, we go out to meet our fate.*

## IF YOU LIKED THIS BOOK...

Escape With Me: A Midlife Love Story

"I gave it all up to be happy. I'd give it all up again for you."

They say life begins after 40, but Cassie ain't feelin' it. Divorced and feeling trapped by her job, she wants to let loose for her friend's tropical beach wedding. She decides to let her hair down and get a little unpredictable. That's when she meets a handsome bartender, Wyatt.

Despite a few grey hairs, Wyatt's the liveliest man that Cassie has ever met. She knows that there's got to be more to his life story than just being a bartender, but this is just supposed to be a vacation fling. And after sunny days spent breaking all the rules on the beach together, Cassie realizes that nobody has ever listened to her the way that Wyatt does.

His carefree life is enviable, his kisses are intoxicating, and she can almost imagine a life with him. But all vacations come to an end. And when Cassie invites him to visit her hometown, Wyatt reveals that he can never go back. Not to her town. Not to America. Not to civilization.

Cassie leaves, confused and heartbroken, wondering just who she got herself involved with. Suddenly, her predictable life gets turned upside down when she sees her picture splashed across the Internet. And when the tabloids come looking for the mature woman who found the lost billionaire, she has no idea what to do...

...until he comes back.

Escape With Me: A Midlife Love Story

## ABOUT THE AUTHOR

New York Times and USA Today Bestseller Krista Lakes is a thirtysomething who recently rediscovered her passion for writing. She is living happily ever after with her Prince Charming. Her first kid just started preschool and she is happy to welcome her second child into her life, continuing her "Happily Ever After"!

Thank you for supporting an indie author. Anything you can do, whether it be writing a review, or even simply telling a fellow reader that you enjoyed this, helps me out immensely. Thanks!

Krista would love to hear from you! Please contact her at Krista.Lakes@gmail.com or friend her on Facebook!

Further reading:

*Bad Boys and Babies*
    Family Doctor's Baby
    The Billionaire's Baby Arrangement
    Crime Boss Baby

*Kinds of Love*
    A Forever Kind of Love
    A Wonderful Kind of Love
    An Endless Kind of Love

*Billionaires and Brides*

Yours Completely: A Cinderella Love Story
Yours Truly: A Cinderella Love Story
Yours Royally: A Cinderella Love Story

*The "Kisses" series*

Saltwater Kisses: A Billionaire Love Story
Kisses From Jack: The Other Side of Saltwater Kisses
Rainwater Kisses: A Billionaire Love Story
Champagne Kisses: A Timeless Love Story
Freshwater Kisses: A Billionaire Love Story
Sandcastle Kisses: A Billionaire Love Story
Hurricane Kisses: A Billionaire Love Story
Barefoot Kisses: A Billionaire Love Story
Sunrise Kisses: A Billionaire Love Story
Waterfall Kisses: A Billionaire Love Story
Island Kisses: A Billionaire Love Story

*Other Novels*

I Choose You: A Secret Billionaire Romance
His Every Desire: A Billionaire Seduction
Wolf Six's Salvation: A Shifter Love Story
Burned: A New Adult Love Story
Walking on Sunshine: A Sweet Summer Romance
An American Cinderella: A Royal Love Story
Mr. Darcy's Kiss: A Contemporary Pride and Prejudice